The Grea

By Ken Balneaves

Published by Ken Balneaves

All characters in this book are fictitious, and any resemblance to actual persons living or dead is purely coincidental.

ISBN 978-0-9571016-0-9

For Sheila with love

1

He had never met his grandfather. In fact no one in the family ever talked about him until his paternal grandmother, on her deathbed, told Richard the sad details of the events that had occurred in his grandfather's life some twenty-three years before.

With enormous pride, his grandmother quietly told that her husband Stuart had been quite an athlete when he was young, a middle distance runner. Her eyes glistened with tears as she spoke affectionately about her husband. Richard listened intently to this, all the while wondering why no one in his family had ever before discussed this with him. Very soon however, he was to learn of his family's dark secret.

"Your grandfather was an extremely handsome man," his grandmother whispered, smiling as she talked, "full of enthusiasm for life, which is why what happened to him, was so terribly tragic, but he made us all promise never to talk about him from the day he left us. It was his choice, not mine," she continued.

"I don't understand." Richard said, thinking that, 'the day he left us' was his grandmother's way of saying, the day he had died.
"Of course, I did see him again you know" said the old woman, completely ignoring Richard's question. "Yes, I did, several times in fact."
Richard was confused by this but permitted her to carry on without his interruption. She spoke more of her husband, saying that he had graduated from Cambridge with a first in Mathematics. Later, he had worked at Oxford University where he lectured in Cosmology achieving much acclaim at the time as an assistant to a well-known and accomplished Cosmologist. However, unbeknown to nearly everyone except his wife, many of the papers published by his mentor were in fact Stuart's own work. This career however was relatively short lived as Stuart decided after a few years that lecturing was not for him after all. He decided this because funding for research in his chosen field was so scarce that he felt he could not do the subject justice and so he made the decision to leave. The old lady continued, telling Richard how Stuart's ill health went undiagnosed by a number of specialists and doctors. Richard also learnt that, following a brief spell of ill health, Stuart had started a business in pharmaceuticals, in 1970.

On hearing this, Richard realised that this was now his dad's and uncle John's business. Until then, he had never known or thought to ask how or when the business began. Richard leant across, touched his grandmother's hand and quietly asked her, "What was wrong with grandfather?"
"No one could tell."

"What were the symptoms then?" he persisted.
The old woman took a deep breath and explained, a tear rolling down one of the creases in her old wrinkled face, just like the first rains in a dry riverbed of the Kalahari. "He sometimes had difficulty breathing and occasionally had to sit down to recover," she said slowly, "they told him he was overdoing the fitness training."
"What was it that actually killed him?" Richard asked rather untactfully.
"My dear, dear boy," she said smiling, looking at him for the first time, "he's not dead, he's merely sleeping." Her voice raising a note at the end of the sentence. At this Richard pulled back slightly and raised an eyebrow. He couldn't make up his mind whether she was telling the truth or she was delusional. As if for confirmation, he glanced across the bed at his mother, who had been silent until then. She had a look of disbelief on her face, however it was not disbelief at what the old lady had said, but that she had said it at all.
"Is this true Mother?" he asked.
"Yes dear, yes it is" she replied hesitantly, adding rather sheepishly, “but I think you should let your Grandmother rest now dear."

Turning to the old lady, Richard’s mother said, “You rest now Irene. James and John will be here to see you by the time you wake up.”
"Why can’t I stay?" asked the young man, now eager to hear more and find out what had happened to his grandfather, the man he had never met and who was never discussed other than in guarded responses to his juvenile questions when he was younger. He now

realised these questions had been parried by his parents and other family members 'in the know'. He was not about to give up now, but before he could ask any more, his grandmother slipped into sleep.
"Let's go Richard," whispered his mother placing her hand lightly on his back and guiding him out of the room.

They left the private side ward to take a break from their vigil. James and his brother John were away on business in Switzerland when Pen took the call from the consultant at the private clinic advising that it was likely to be a matter of hours, not days, as they had previously been told, before their mother passed away. Following the call, Richard and Pen had rushed straight to the clinic calling James en-route. James and John had booked flights immediately and were now expected to arrive at the hospital in about half an hour.

Richard and his mother had a coffee in the visitors' lounge before returning to the side ward where they sat with his sleeping grandmother until his father and uncle arrived. Richard's mother desperately wanted to let her husband know what his mother had told Richard, but the opportunity did not arise, as when the two men arrived they immediately walked into the side ward.

They all sat round the bed with the old lady's sons holding a hand each, waiting for her to wake which she did, almost on cue and looked at James who instantly said, "Hello Mum, I'm here, so is John."
"I know," she replied weakly "you all are; your father is too". Richard's father looked at his wife who gave a

troubled smile that told him everything. He looked at Richard who nodded and raised his mouth into a smile that didn't reach his eyes and said, "She told me about my Grandfather. Dad, why didn't you?"
"Not now son, not now," he replied as he looked back towards his mother. The old lady was rambling, talking about old friends and past events as though they were happening for her at the present moment. Suddenly she strained to raise her head and looked at the back wall of the room saying, "Oh Stuart, it's so good to see you. My, how handsome you look. It's as though you never left." They all looked round to see who was there, but no-one was and as they looked back the old lady drew her final breath and passed away. One of the attending doctors walked over to her bedside and checked her pulse. Finding that there wasn't one, he bowed his head and pronounced her dead at 4:30 p.m.

After a few moments observing the old lady, Richard's father leant over and closed her eyelids. They all sat there in silence looking at her again at peace at last after her long, and sometimes painful, battle with cancer.

Richard, whilst extremely upset at her passing, was also thinking that it was now his mother and father's responsibility to fill in the rest of the details relating to what his grandmother had said about his grandfather, the man he never knew. One thing was for certain, he was determined to seek out his grandfather, whether or not his family approved.

2

Richard Harper, an only child, had just started at Cambridge University where he was reading Cosmology after passing his A-levels with four straight 'A's. He was considered to be an exceptionally gifted student and was expected to achieve a first class honours degree. Like his parents and, he had just learned, his grandfather, he was also a very keen sportsman taking it all extremely seriously and indeed he excelled at it; a natural sportsman with a powerful sculpted physique. He trained regularly and was extremely fit. His specialist area in sport was rowing the single scull.

Weekdays, Richard lived in a rented flat in Cambridge conveniently located close to the University. At the weekend he travelled to the St John's Wood penthouse flat in London, owned by his parents, so he could be close to their London home in Acacia Road, just round the corner. His parents were in London frequently due to his father's business commitments. Allowing Richard to have the flat was their way of giving Richard his freedom, but ensuring that he maintained his contact with them no matter whether he was in Cambridge or in London. His mother was particularly concerned that he would throw himself into work and sport far too much unless forced to take a break. She considered that she needed to be on hand to oversee that; he disagreed but loved the flat. They knew he was young to have such freedom but they trusted him to treat the flat with respect, after all, they knew him to be a sensible and level headed boy.

Richard's parents were extremely enthusiastic about sport and that had undoubtedly been the cause of Richard's own great interest. In his youth they had been very supportive of anything he wanted to try, but without being pushy. They had been great sports achievers themselves so they were not trying to live their sports lives through him, thus his interest was self developed with assistance rather than being forced. Richard was grateful for this approach, as, over the years, he had seen many of his friends drop by the wayside when parents failed to realise that they could not compel their children to be good at sport.

His father, James Harper, was a runner, and had been a middle distance champion when he was at Oxford. After University, where James studied as a Chemist, he entered into the family business with his father and brother John, researching and producing new drugs.The fact of his grandfather's involvement in the founding of the business was something Richard had only recently been made aware of. His mother had been at Guys Hospital where she studied and became a doctor. She too was a keen sportswoman; she had excelled in Hockey, playing for the England 1st team in her day.

Richard's parents had met on a skiing holiday in 1980 in Val D'isère. They had each travelled with a number of friends and had met in an après ski bar in the resort. Both being of a medical background they hit it off immediately and it was a great surprise to them both to find that, not only were they from the same city, they in fact lived within a mile of each other in Cambridge. They continued to see each other when they returned from their skiing trip and, as they say, the rest is history. Richard had heard this story on numerous occasions and was quietly rather envious of his parents' apparent ease with each other when they first met. He, on the other hand, despite being a very handsome young man with wavy black hair and deep blue eyes found that kind of thing a bit of challenge, a bit difficult, embarrassing even. This was so much of a problem for him that he had developed a stutter which embarrasingly emerged when he was in the company of females of his own age. However, the stutter aside, it was hardly surprising he could not relate to women given his dedication to school work, and now university studies, over the past few years.

During the next week, the mood at home was extremely solemn. There was little conversation going on and James was struggling to contain his emotions, which was upsetting for his wife and for Richard as his father's sorrow spilt over. Richard and his mother had their own grief, but somehow James's seemed to add to it. Nonetheless, the family went about making the necessary arrangements for Irene's funeral, the silence being broken from time to time by telephone calls and the odd visit to their home by friends and family wishing to convey their condolences and by the undertaker and the vicar.

For Richard, the day of the funeral passed extremely slowly; each minute seemed to drag. It was of course a dreadfully sad day, but as most of the mourners' commented, it was a blessed relief for the old lady who had been in pain from the cancer for such a long time. Richard and his parents headed home when the wake ended, thoroughly exhausted. The silence in their car was audible, each of them with their own private thoughts.

The following day they sat down with Richard to explain the family's dark secret. His uncle John would join them in the discussion. As John arrived, the four of them moved to the lounge and sat on the sofas, Richard sitting forward on the front of his seat, edgy, similar to an accused man about to have a sentence passed upon him. However, over the next hour or so, the family opened up about his grandfather.

Richard learnt that Stuart Harper was born on 22nd January 1932, in Oxford, England. He knew from his grandmother that his grandfather had studied at Cambridge University and little else but by the end of the frank and open discussion, his parents and his uncle had filled in most of the gaps in his knowledge. What Richard was most anxious to understand of course was what had happened to him, was he dead or not?

In 1971, Stuart had been diagnosed with Motor Neurone Disease or MND for short, which Richard knew to be a progressively degenerative condition affecting the ability to control voluntary muscle activity, eventually affecting the ability to speak, walk, breath, swallow and generally move the body. This diagnosis was confirmed when his old ailments, those which his grandmother referred to before she died, were revisited and specialists realised that his previously undiagnosed issues were in fact the early onset of this disease and the reason he was forced to curtail his fitness training.

His father explained, "Despite his affliction, until 1975, your grandfather was able to feed himself and get in and out of bed. Your grandmother managed to help him and to bring up John and me, without outside help. But shortly after that he deteriorated dramatically, to the point where he was unable to do anything for himself and was wheelchair bound. He could still talk, just, but even that was about to give up. In 1978 he needed to have a tracheotomy operation and from then on required 24 hour nursing care. However, before the operation, which was required to enable him to continue breathing, he told the family that he wanted to go to a care home and for the sake of the business he wanted them to have no contact with him from then on."

Richard gasped in disbelief and sat even further forward than he had been as his father continued. "We were of course completely shocked and upset, but his reasoning was that the business was doing very well by then and he figured that it was ironic that he dealt in the field of pharmaceuticals but could not come up with a drug to treat himself. He thought, somewhat irrationally I have to say, that this could be damaging for the business, so he decided that he should have no further part of it, leaving it to John and me to look after your grandmother, and insisting that he should be incarcerated in a home."

Pen could see that explaining all of this was very difficult for her husband, perhaps as he was talking about his newly deceased mother. She moved to sit next to him, put her hand on his and squeezed gently.

"Although he loved us all dearly, particularly your grandmother, he wanted the family to leave him to the care of the home without any further contact; he could see no point as his condition was beginning to leave him completely helpless and unable to communicate. He told us we had no part in this decision, as he would not give us Power of Attorney unless we agreed. Reluctantly, and with much wrangling and upset we did agree."

"So what happened to him?" asked Richard demandingly, unable to contain himself any longer.
"That was twenty-three years ago," his father continued, "and no one has been to see him since. We do get reports; he is still alive but only just, he has no ability to move. John and I have run the business ever since and have looked after your grandmother financially. We have also paid for all the costs of keeping your grandfather in the care home; he is comfortable there, or as comfortable as they can make him given his condition. He almost has no communication with anyone now."

"Where is he, I want to see him," demanded Richard. "He's in a home in the countryside in Yorkshire," said John, "he was moved there a few years ago as the air is better than in the London home he was in." "Did you see him then?" Richard asked.
"No we just agreed to the move and paid for it, we were respecting his wishes," his mother replied. "That's very harsh Mother, I want to see him," Richard said, scolding her.
"Your grandfather doesn't even know of your existence, Richard," said his father.
"Exactly," retorted Richard, "I want to see him." "The shock might kill him," said his mother.

"It sounds to me like he's already dead as far as you're concerned and what kind of a life must he have? I want to see him," Richard repeated in a raised voice. He was furious that his parents could have agreed to such a thing, but he was told he was young and didn't fully understand. Richard got up and walked out, saying: "If you won't tell me where he is I will just have to find him myself."

On the first day of the Easter break, Richard set himself the task of doing just that, but at the last minute his mother relented and told him his grandfather's location. Richard set out that morning to drive to Yorkshire to visit his grandfather. He arrived at the nursing home just before three o'clock when they were handing out tea. The home, a magnificent old building in a private estate with many acres of grounds, was like a five star hotel with nursing staff instead of waiters. He parked his father's car, which he had commandeered for the trip, and entered the building by walking up the few stone steps to the reception area. There were two smartly dressed young women on the desk that appeared to be not much older than him. One of them looked up as he approached the desk.

"Can I help you, Sir?" she asked politely.

"Y-y-yes," he blurted out in embarrassment as the young woman smiled at him. "I, I, I'm here to s-s-see S-Stuart Harper," he continued, aware that he was blushing and wishing that the receptionist had been a Matron or perhaps a man even; anything but this. The two receptionists were now looking at him obviously admiring his good looks as one commented that no one had ever visited Stuart Harper since he came to the home.

"He, he's my g-g-grandfather."

This wasn't easy for him, but one of the receptionists smiled and told Richard to follow her and she directed him to where his grandfather was. As Richard turned away the two girls looked at each other and tilted their heads giving each other a knowing look of pity for Richard's embarrassment. His guide moved to pass Richard, saying, "Please follow me, Sir." Which he did; trying not to look at the pretty girl's legs as she walked ahead of him.

"There he is," she said at the door of a large room, pointing to a man in a wheelchair.

"Th-th-thank you," he stammered.

His grandfather was in the TV room. He was apparently always in the TV room in front of the Discovery Channel just sitting and being fed by one of his personal nurses. As he approached, Richard was particularly pleased to see that this nurse was much older than him. He took a

deep breath to compose himself and he slowly walked up to the old man, observing him only at first from the rear then walking round to the side and then the front. The nurse looked up from the food and asked him what he wanted.
"Can he hear me?" Richard asked, ignoring her question.
"Yes," she said, "but who are you?"
Again he ignored her and said, "Hello Grandfather, I'm Richard Harper, your son James' son."
The old man didn't move at all but the nurse said, "He knows you're here."
"How do you know?" questioned Richard.
"He has eye movement," she responded, "and a move acknowledges what is said."
"So he can communicate," said Richard, "please teach me the signs; I want to get to know him." "There aren't many signs," she replied, now accepting his presence, "just left for 'no', right for 'yes' and up for 'I want something'".
"What about down?" enquired Richard excited that he would be able to communicate with his grandfather.
"There isn't a down. Or at least if there is his head is so low now you wouldn't be able to see it," she replied.

Over the next hour or so Richard, with the initial assistance of the nurse, 'talked' with his grandfather. It was slow going but quite an achievement. After a while the nurse, who had diplomatically retired earlier, came back and told Richard that the old man was now very tired and that he should leave. Richard asked a final question as to whether his grandfather would like him to come back again. His grandfather sat for a few moments, and then moved his eyes to the right. Richard squeezed his grandfather's hand warmly and said, "See you soon, Grandad". As Richard departed, a tear ran down the old man's left cheek, but no-one noticed.

Realising that communication in this way was difficult for his grandfather Richard turned his mind to developing a way to make it easier for him. Perhaps there was a computer that could detect eye movement. He researched this and became aware that in America others with MND had equipment that could detect the smallest movement of the eye. That might mean the old man would not tire so easily. Richard sourced the computer and software and persuaded his father to purchase it and this allowed him much quicker and more meaningful communication with his grandfather.

A switch operated by eye movement controlled the program. When Stuart had built up what he wanted to say, he sent it to a speech synthesizer. This was still a relatively slow process at up to only 20 words a minute but effective and the synthesized voice was readily recognisable and unique to his grandfather.

3

Over the next year, Richard was a regular companion for the old man and learnt much from him, particularly relating to his past achievements with his research projects when he had first started at Oxford University and had been an assistant to a world famous cosmologist. Naturally, as a junior member of staff, his many achievements had been attributed to the department's more senior members in charge of the research; nevertheless he knew what he had achieved and that was what was important to him.

The old man helped Richard with his studies at Cambridge and helped him excel in what was now his second year. The breadth of Richard's knowledge and depth of his understanding astounded his university lecturers. He was simply way beyond the level of his peers and was soon receiving firm offers for research posts commencing immediately after his graduation.

During the years that Richard's grandfather had been isolated, research and technology had taken a massive surge forward. However, as a result of his constantly watching the Discovery Channel, Stuart had kept abreast of a good number of the advancements made in his field. He was also aware that there were recent advances in communication techniques operated directly by the mind with a special cap that had electrodes, which pressed into the scalp and linked to a computer. Richard and his grandfather discussed this and Richard again persuaded his father to purchase the equipment. After a few weeks of training this allowed Stuart to talk through the computer as fast as he could think which was sometimes so fast that Richard had trouble keeping up.

Initially the speech was synthesised, but Richard dug out an old radio interview with his grandfather on it when he was in his late thirties, before the tracheotomy. He had the speech pattern analysed and a programme developed so his grandfather could speak through the computer using his own speech, which was a vast improvement on the digital version and this somehow drew Richard even closer to the old man. They discussed the Natural History TV programmes on the Discovery Channel, which for years Stuart had been silently taking in. The absence of distractions at the care home had allowed Stuart to refine his ideas about human thought processes to an extremely high level. Richard also learned that his grandfather's passion, in fact his obsession, was theoretical physics and the passage of time. Richard was completely unaware of the ways in which his intervention would enable his grandfather to refine and develop these ideas to an extent that their application by Richard would fundamentally change what it meant to be human.

The more he got to know his grandfather the more Richard understood the reasons behind his wish to be left at the nursing home with no contact from family members. He realised the old man was an unselfish individual who did not want to burden his family with his affliction. He wanted them to be free from his life dictating the pace and direction of their lives. However, things were different now; he could communicate again and following discussions with his family Richard took his grandfather out of the home to another one that was close to his Cambridge flat. In fact he would have liked to have had him at home, but realised that was completely out of the question, given the round-the-clock care he required.

Everyone was pleased by the move; not least his grandfather who now had a new lease of life and the challenge of guiding Richard through the last year of his degree and subsequently through a Masters that, with his grandfather's help, he achieved in record time. Following the completion of Richard's studies, his grandfather returned to his own research. Richard, who by now was an assistant to some of the country's best researchers in the field of natural science and cosmology, arranged for his grandfather to have a research post at Cambridge. For the next few years they worked together and published many papers on the basic laws that govern the universe, Einstein's General Theory of Relativity and the theory that implied space and time would have a beginning in the Big Bang and an end in black holes and on the possible developments of String Theory and multidimensional space.

In 2010, Richard's grandfather finally received the acclaim he deserved when the Queen knighted him for his services to research. It was a proud moment for the entire family and one that none, save for Richard, had ever so much as dreamt of. Stuart was proud also, but rather sad that his wife Irene could not have been there to see it. The death of his son John in a tragic and freak accident in 2003 had also been a sad loss for the old man. John had been on holiday with his wife in St. Maarten in the Virgin Islands when a hurricane struck their hotel. They had been warned to stay indoors which they apparently did, but the metal roof of their chalet bedroom lifted in the violent winds allowing the walls to collapse directly on top of where they were taking refuge. They were both killed outright.

Stuart was delighted with his Knighthood, "Sir Stuart Harper," he said as he left the presence of the Queen, "it has a ring to it does it not?"
"It does indeed, Grandad, it does indeed." Richard replied laughing as he pushed his grandfather's wheelchair along the deep pile red carpet.
As they walked through the doors of the Palace, there was rapturous applause from the large gathered crowd. The family, who were all there to see the ceremony, looked back and up thinking the Queen must have come out onto the balcony. She was not there. Richard then said, "This is for you, Grandad, the people love you. You have made it and deservedly so." At this tears started to run down Pen's cheeks and even James could not hold back the moisture from his eyes. They waved on behalf of the old man who seemed to be smiling, something he had not managed for many a year, as they

got into the specially adapted limousine. Soon they were driving slowly off to their London home.

Once there, James reflected on the day with Richard. He too was sad that his brother John could not have been there. His thoughts turned to the time when he had sold the business. It was 2005, two years after his brother died. James had felt that the business was not the same after John died, it wasn't fun anymore. It had been an extremely lucrative business and he considered himself very fortunate that it permitted him to retire at forty-six. Selling up was not a decision he made lightly, but after it became clear that Richard would not follow in his footsteps, and with no one else in the running to take over, it seemed like the right decision. It was however a great regret that his brother was not around to reap the rewards of their combined efforts. It did leave James extremely wealthy, as they had discovered many life-changing drugs over the years, so there were several patents to sell with the company.
James' thoughts drifted to his father and the elusive drug that could have helped him. It never came, despite continuing research in that area.

Coming back out of his reverie James heard his father tell Richard that he expected him to be the next one in the family to be awarded an accolade from the Queen in 2012 after the Olympic Games that were being held in London. Richard was expected to represent Britain in the single scull. His grandfather was extremely proud of this as he remembered when he had been a contender to represent his country but sadly had been prevented from taking part by the ill health that was a precursor to his being diagnosed with MND. Nevertheless, he was really supportive of his grandson who by then would be twenty-nine and at his peak of performance and fitness and was expected to take Gold for Britain.

Unhappily, it was not to be that Stuart would ever see that day as by Christmas 2011 his MND symptoms had increased markedly. His condition had reached a stage where his eyes were continually closed. He had become completely motionless to the point where it was impossible to detect whether he was still alive, save that his computer continued to talk under his silent and motionless control. No amount of medical intervention could halt the condition this time and Stuart died at his care home on 22nd January 2012, exactly four score years to the day from when he was born.

From an outsider's point of view, Stuart appeared to have been a rather sad character, although he would have disagreed. He considered himself to be lucky because his condition progressed far more slowly than was usual, many sufferers dying shortly after they contracted the disease. Undoubtedly, as a result of his condition and the inability to do anything other than think, his mind was immeasurably more developed than the average genius. With the severity of his condition keeping him motionless and with his eyes closed it was not surprising that at his passing no one noticed. It was in fact some time before his carers realised that he had passed on. The peculiar thing is that for the two hours or so that Stuart sat there, dead in his wheelchair, his computer continued to speak softly and therefore also record what was being said. This was unnoticed at the time. None of the family was around and his carers had left him to sleep, but the time of death had been confirmed at the inquest as being 1 p.m. Richard realised that there was a time lapse beyond when his grandfather was clinically dead and when the computer stopped being under his control, during which time, Stuart, through his computer, had continued to speak. Richard knew that during his lifetime, Stuart had in private dabbled with the possibilities of an afterlife. He had never made his thoughts public other than to Richard, who had been rather dismissive of this prospect, preferring to concentrate on the here and now of cosmology. Now he was beginning to wonder whether the old man had been right after all.

In his chosen field of work, Richard's curiosity was inexorable. He needed to explore the possibility that his grandfather was controlling the computer beyond his clinical death. But, being a scientist, he knew that even if this were true, if he stated it to the scientific world he would face ridicule. 'The computer clock was wrong' or 'he pre-recorded the speech and, before he died, set the computer to converse.' He could hear the doubters now. He had learnt this from his grandfather when he was recounting new discoveries, so he knew that scientists encounter this sort of scepticism all the time. He needed to research the possibility and bide his time before releasing this; if it were true that is; and that was a big 'if'. After all, was it really possible that his grandfather controlled a computer after his clinical death? And if so, did what he said make sense? He needed to take this slowly. At the inquest, required because Stuart was in a care home, the Coroner had reached a verdict of death by natural causes and NMD as was entirely expected. However, Richard's own inquest into his grandfather's computer was to prove to be less straightforward. After carefully backing up the hard drive in the privacy of the study of his Cambridge flat, Richard started to review the text files that drove the speech synthesizer that were time stamped just before and after the clinical death time.

In spite of his intense sadness at the loss of his grandfather, mentor and, by now, great friend, being a scientist, he was completely open-minded towards what he would find. However, nothing could have prepared him for what he was about to discover and to his astonishment he found himself extremely nervous at the prospect of seeing and hearing words written by the mind of a dead man. After sorting the files sequentially he calculated the total talk time to be about 10 hours with an hour before the time of death and the rest after it. This severely challenged Richard, as the time available for recording was only about two hours so how could 11 hours of files be possible he wondered. In an effort to understand, he proceeded, opening the first file and reading the text version rather than listening to it. It made harrowing reading. It seemed the old man was alone and frightened at the end. The words were very similar to anyone else at the end of their life with the usual rambling thoughts, welcomes to old friends etc., but there were also cries for someone to help him. Sadly, it appeared that no one had heard him, possibly the volume on the computer was set too low. Richard was distraught. To think that he had not been there for his grandfather at the end brought him to tears. He thought the old man must have been so frightened and alone. For him to have dealt with his disabilities in such a brave and dismissing way for almost his entire life and in the final throes of life to be reduced to this was almost more than Richard could stand. He sat back from the screen and cried hard, completely overcome by the emotion he was experiencing. The tears were cascading down his young cheeks so much that he could no longer read. After a few minutes, he leant forward and switched the computer off and retired to his bedroom. Still desperately upset, he sobbed himself to sleep.

In the morning he was awoken by the sunshine searing through the slight gap between curtains like shards of glass from a broken pane, straight into Richard's sore, red eyes. Irritated by the imposition, he pulled the covers over his head. He started thinking of his grandfather again which made him restless so he rose, showered and dressed quickly. He could not however keep his mind free from thought of what his grandfather would have done in his position. Answering his own question out loud, he said "He would have been unable to prevent his enquiring nature getting the better of him, that's what." Richard reached for the telephone to call work to tell them he would not be in as he was too upset. After making the call he sat back on the sofa and reflected for a while thinking the situation through before looking at the remainder of his grandfather's file. However, he missed his grandfather's computer generated voice so much that he thought he would play the files through the Synthesizer. After all, he lived alone so there was no likelihood of his being disturbed on a Monday. Richard prepared a coffee and some toast then settled himself in front of his multimedia system ready to play the files. Apprehensively, he told the computer to play the first file that was recorded just after his grandfather's death. The file began and at first there was nothing to hear except white noise. Just as Richard was about to tell the computer to fast forward, suddenly, grabbing his attention, a synthesized voice said: "Richard". Richard nearly fell off his seat for by now the recording was two minutes after the official time of death. Not sure whether he had heard it or imagined it, he told the computer to rewind the file by thirty seconds. Again he heard it just when he expected to, "Richard .... yes it is me and I am fine. Very dead in your understanding of the word but fine none the less, please don't upset yourself, don't worry about me. You see I am in the next stage of being, beyond life as we knew it; it does exist, the after life."

Richard's heart was racing. Was he really listening to his grandfather, after his death? So many questions were rising in his mind when the voice said, "I know you will doubt that this is really me but I assure you it is, I am with you, we all are, everyone that has died, only not in being." He continued, "It is as I thought. Here, time goes forwards and backwards so we know what is coming, but time has little relevance as we can pass back and forth at will. We can also see your world; look out of the window, there is a small brown dog crossing the road without a care for the red Mercedes that is speeding towards him. The car won't hit the dog, but it will be close."

Richard got up immediately, opened the French doors and walked onto the balcony that overlooked the road outside. He looked over the handrail to see exactly what had been described just as a red car squealed to a halt narrowly missing a small brown dog, exactly as had been described by the voice. The dog yelped and ran off into the adjacent park. Richard spun round and rushed back into the room closing the doors behind him.

"B-b-but h-how did you know?" Richard exclaimed as he locked the doors. He was not expecting an answer, but to his utter amazement he got one. "I told you I can see your world," the voice said. Half thinking he was going mad Richard said: "B-but how am I holding a c-conversation with a r-recording?" The stutter betraying his stress level.

"Well," the voice continued, "you remember that the first two minutes of this recording were blank. That was when I was getting to know where I now am. Your two minutes is an eternity for me but not an unpleasant eternity in the context we sometimes used to use the word. With time running forwards or backwards, I know exactly what you are going to say and when, so my answers are pre-empting your questions. Even if you try to fool me by pausing, I know that too, so I compensate in my text."

"Richard" continued the voice, "do you recall the diagram showing singularity?"

"Y-yes," said Richard "of c-course I do."

"Then you will recall that it is like a world globe where the North and South Poles have been pulled apart to form something reminiscent of an American football, but with the points being sharpened to infinity," said his

grandfather. "The South Pole is the point of the Big Bang, a singularity, the start of time as we know it and the universe expands to the equator of the ball and will recede as it passes this mid-point to, ultimately, a second singularity at the North Pole where I believed time would pass through the point of infinity again and beyond. I believed that anything was possible beyond that point including time going backwards, but in your time it will be many millions of years before you can know that for certain. But life is very similar to this theory. It starts with a Big Bang, if you will pardon the expression, and the individual expands or grows until a certain time when their life begins to ebb, in small ways to start with, loss of fitness, aches and pains and wrinkles but more seriously with poor health and diseases as we reach our 'North Pole'."
Richard was dumbstruck, listening to his grandfather's voice because he suddenly realised again that he was listening to the words of a man that had passed on half-an-hour or so before this point in the file. Regaining his composure slightly, he reached over for a pad to make notes of thoughts that occurred to him as his grandfather talked, so that he could ask questions later.

His grandfather continued, "At the North Pole, just before you die, it is very tight, you cannot breathe as you feel you are being pushed backwards into a tunnel, the reverse of being born with the light at the end of the tunnel being very bright at first then fainter and fainter. Just as you feel you are going to suffocate, you die and move on to the next phase of being..."
Richard, realising Stuart had paused, sat bolt upright and blurted out, "Is-is that when you called out for help,

was it f-frightening? Were you scared when no one came? I'm-I'm sorry, I should have been there."

"Stop now, don't fret," said his grandfather, "it was terrifying at the time, but now I am at such peace, all is wonderful, the motionless, twisted body I had in my past life is gone and I am free to be as everyone and everything else is."

"That's absolutely wonderful, Grandad, but what do you mean 'and everything else is'?" said Richard, returning to his curious self and losing the stutter, with his reducing stress.

"Well," said his grandfather, "it's not only us humans that are here, there are animals and plants too."

"But how? What form do they take in the afterlife?"

His grandfather told him that it was unimportant; at which point Richard stood up and almost shouted at his sound system, "How can it be unimportant? You are telling me that there is an after-life, not only for humans and animals, but for plants too; something that no one else has ever proved before and you say it's unimportant? This is The Holy Grail, what everyone has been looking for since time began. You must tell me everything."

"My dear boy, please don't upset yourself. There is much you could not possibly comprehend; I did not, and could not have in the previous part of my life, but I do now. To give you a simplistic insight that you will understand, it is akin to every being, plant or creature, that ever lived being an atom in a larger entity but still being a whole in itself. It is not the Holy Grail because it is not holy. There is no religion here, no race, no disease or disfigurement, no aggression, no crime and no death. Similar to the universe, it is ever expanding with no boundaries and time is no barrier. You will eventually experience it for yourself." His grandfather paused and then said, "In the meantime, I have something very important for you to do for your world, that will change your life and those of others forever."

4

Richard by now was unbelievably confused, but nevertheless transfixed and without realising it he had been sitting all tensed up as if he was a cornered cat. Slowly, he untensed his muscles, dropped his shoulders and assumed a more relaxed position on the couch as his grandfather continued.

"As you know my IQ was one of the highest that man or woman has ever achieved, yours is similar. We nonetheless use only about ten percent of our brainpower and to date no one has managed to use much more than that. It has been impossible for us to harness, much like a computer hard drive with sticky tape on ninety percent of the disc. Do you agree?"

"Yes," Richard said slowly.

"We are blighted during our lifetime by disease and illnesses that cause premature death. Sometimes our bodies give out on us yet scientists have proven that humans in your phase of life have the ability to live for up to 1,000 years. However, this has been particularly elusive, although it has been less so for some trees that have already lived a life that long or indeed longer. Also, some animals outlive humans such as Harriet, a giant Galapagos land tortoise, she is about 170 years old now, and a clam was recently discovered that is believed to have lived for about four hundred years. This longevity has however escaped every human and until recently where people are living into their eighties and nineties, three score years and ten was pretty much the norm although there has been the odd exception such as Jeanne Calment, a French woman. She died in 1997, at 122 years of age."

"Yes, I remember that, we discussed it at school," interrupted Richard, "I was fourteen then and was amazed that she was 108 years older than me. I wondered what it would be like to live that long."

"Well," continued his grandfather "it can be like that and I am going to teach you all how to access the remaining ninety percent of your brain and how to live longer, much longer. You will still die, but if you are careful, not until you are ready and not until you have fulfilled your wildest dreams in terms of learning and knowledge."

"If I am careful?" enquired Richard.

"Yes," replied his grandfather, "I am not suggesting immortality, you can still die accidentally as you are all still flesh and bone, but illness, disease and pestilence will be a thing of the past.

Richard had his mouth open; even with his superior IQ he had his mouth open. Here he was being given the opportunity to be the bearer of knowledge to permit every human being on earth to live almost forever.

"Tell me please," he said, "I must know now."

"Not quite yet," said his grandfather, "first you have to be prepared."

"H-how," said Richard suddenly becoming nervous, "what do you mean?"

His grandfather continued: "You don't know much about hypnosis do you?"
"No, I don't. I..."
His grandfather cut in: "That was a rhetorical question. I know you don't know, I've seen your lack of knowledge on the subject. Next week, at my funeral on Wednesday, you will meet a young woman who will change that. Her name is Helen Harrison and she is one of the country's leading authorities on hypnosis and hypnotherapy. When you meet, she will be pleased to discuss the concept with you and you must learn as much as you can from her. Do not at this stage mention what we have discussed here today. Also bear in mind that if you listen to this file again, it will not be interactive as the time for you has gone. You will still hear my voice but it would not make sense to anyone else as it will not be interactive and they are likely to be sceptical as a result. When you have learnt about hypnotherapy, come back and listen to the next part of this file."
"When?" blurted out Richard realising that his grandfather was about to stop talking on this file. "Whenever you are ready my boy," came the reply, "I will be here."
"But what if I change my mind on the time, maybe the day after, maybe not?"
"No matter, Richard, no matter. I will be here when you are ready. Remember, I have seen your life backwards so I will be here. Goodbye, my boy."
Richard immediately replied, "If you have seen my life, when will I......" There was a click. "die?" He knew he was no longer listening to the file as he recognised the sound of the multimedia system swapping over to the

radio as it said, *'This is the BBC news on Monday the 30th January at twelve midday.'* The presenter paused and then commenced with *'The funeral of Sir Stuart Harper the theoretical physicist who died last Sunday 22nd January, is to take place on Wednesday 8th February. The burial will be at the family plot in Oxford following a service to be held at Downing College Chapel at Cambridge University. The family has chosen the venue for the diverse community of people of different faiths who use this chapel, and for the many who are not practising members of any religion. They have asked that mourners do not send flowers but if they wish to, should make donations to The Motor Neuron Disease Association (UK).'* The presenter paused again. *'Economic indicators for last year rose by ten percent, says the Governor of the ...* "System off", Richard shouted. The room was plunged into a deep silence. Richard had so many unanswered questions. He looked at the notepad on his knee but there was no writing on the page; so surprised was he by the content of the file that he had been transfixed and had written nothing at all. His mind was spinning. He had just listened to, no, conversed with, a computer file, for over an hour. Was it his grandfather? Twice the file had correctly predicted future events, first the dog nearly being run over and again with the day of his grandfather's funeral that, until the radio broadcast he had just heard, had not been announced. 'Am I going mad,' he thought to himself. He felt he needed to talk to someone. He picked up the phone and was about to reconnect the cable that he had earlier unplugged when he remembered his grandfather's instructions, 'Do not at this stage mention what we have discussed here today.' He put the phone down again.

That afternoon Richard decided that he should go to the gym as he had missed his normal training session at the Riversedge Club over the weekend. Indeed since the death of his grandfather he had not found the will to train. He constantly found himself sitting on the equipment staring into space thinking about what had happened. Friends and staff asked him how he was, but he looked through them in a daze, barely able to return a word. Fortunately, they put it down to his loss, which was partly true as Richard was indeed hurting at the passing of his grandfather. He was just beginning to take in what his grandfather could be offering with massive mental powers and vastly increased life span, the genesis of a new age. Could it be true? He had never doubted the 'Master' before. As he sat in the gym, his thoughts ran through the possibilities of what was on offer, when it suddenly dawned on him that his grandfather would never be a part of it despite being the architect. This realisation saddened him tremendously, so much so that he felt he needed to be on his own, unable to be even slightly communicative and certainly not sufficiently so to be around other people. He left the gym quickly without changing and returned home.

Back at the flat Richard was sorely tempted to listen to the next file, but he then thought that there were only so many files and perhaps the time might be wasted if he did not first do what his grandfather had asked of him. On the other hand, he thought his grandfather would know that he would return before gaining the knowledge about hypnosis and would be expecting him. He was in turmoil. This was all so surreal. However, after a while, with his scientist's head on, he managed to contain his urge until he had the opportunity of gaining the necessary knowledge relating to hypnosis. After all, his grandfather had often chastised him in the past for not being fully prepared before making a decision, an impulsive tendency he was keen to overcome as he knew it was not conducive to good research and reporting. Confused and upset, instead of going to the next file he distracted himself with TV, watching some news before going to bed at around ten p.m. It had been a long and tiring day.

The next few days seemed endless for Richard and by Saturday he was constantly struggling to keep himself from listening to the next file. Even so, after a good workout at the gym, where this time he was more willing and able to talk to friends and staff, he retired to his flat for a well-earned rest. He slept well that night for the first time since his grandfather's death. He was awakened at ten a.m. by the sound of church bells ringing in the morning service. Richard didn't attend church; he never had except when forced to as a child by his parents. They never went to church themselves; a family friend who was an Elder at the church always took Richard and his own son. At the time, Richard thought nothing of it, but as he grew up and thought about those days, he suspected that it was his parents' way of getting 'quality time' with each other without him being there. Initially he resented them pushing him away every week, but now he understood the situation.

It made him smile when he thought about it, which was pretty much every weekend when he heard the bells toll. As he thought of his parents, he decided to call his mother to see if she had any knowledge of hypnotherapy.
"Hello Mother," he said formally as she took the call, "it's me."
"Oh Richard, it's good to hear from you, how are you darling?"
"I'm very well Mum. What about you and Dad?"
"Oh, we're fine too. We're just planning our next cruise, but I'm pleased you called; I was going to call you, but perhaps now you have you can come across for dinner this afternoon."
Richard loved his mother's cooking; in fact he sometimes wondered why he didn't take advantage of it more often when they were actually in Cambridge.
"Thanks, I'd love to. See you at the normal time?" asked Richard.
"Yes darling, see you at four," replied his mother. She was a stickler for timekeeping when it came to meals. If the family members were not at the table when it was ready she would become most exasperated, not something Richard liked to bring about, as he knew the consequences.

After the call, Richard spent some time sitting in his lounge in front of the multimedia system researching hypnosis and hypnotherapy on the Internet and through the University Intranet. He found vast amounts of information on the subject, but also an even greater quantity of contrary opinion that decried the practice as being complete bunkum. 'That is so often the case with Internet searches', he thought. Even narrowing the search down, Richard had difficulty in gaining any worthwhile information upon which he felt he could rely. He therefore decided to wait until the funeral when he had been told he would meet Helen Harrison to see if she could be more informative, after all, his grandfather had assured him she would be. Richard looked at the clock, it was five minutes to four and he suddenly remembered he should be at his parent's place by now. He immediately left and sprinted the few hundred metres to their house. His father greeted him at the door.

"Hello son, you're pushing your luck aren't you? It's nearly four o'clock."

"Hi Dad, yes I know, I'm researching something at present and I forgot the time," replied Richard, only slightly out of breath from the run.

"Well, you're here now, quick, hands washed and to the table, or it's the naughty step for you." His dad laughed heartily. Richard quickly went to the cloakroom to wash his hands and just as he came out his mother shouted "Dinner's ready". Richard thought 'that was close' as they all sat down to eat and his dad winked at him. Richard smiled back.

"So, Richard..." both his mother and father said together. They both stopped and looked at each other.

"I was going to ask what Richard was working on now that needed information on hypnotherapy," said his mother.

"I was going to ask him what he was researching today," said his father.

"I'm researching hypnotherapy for a project that grandfather left unfinished," Richard said in response to them both, not really wanting to tell them more at this stage but realising he should expand slightly.
"I need to understand how it works; can you help me on that Mum?"
"Not really darling, it wasn't a subject we covered at Medical School, I did know one or two people who were reading it, but it was considered rather a controversial alternative treatment method in my day."
"Have either of you ever been hypnotised?" Richard asked.
"Yes, we both have," said his mother, "but only for fun when we were entertained on board one of the cruises we were on a few years ago. Or rather we became the entertainment. Fortunately one of our friends captured it on the camcorder otherwise we would not have believed that we could be so extrovert on stage, of all places, with half the ship watching."
"Yes," added Richard's father, "we were famous for days on board after that episode everyone recognised us and told us how funny we had been."
"Hmm," muttered Richard, not impressed by his parents' embarrassing moment, "not quite what I was after."
They both laughed at his shocked response, teasing him slightly over his reserve. Richard suspected he was not too far wrong in what it was that they would not have normally done. They said they had been pounced upon by the hypnotist to take part as they sat quietly in the audience. His dad playfully blamed his mum's poor vision which meant they were sitting at the front so were an easy target. His mum blamed his dad for

wearing a cream suit, saying that was the real reason they had been chosen.

As Richard's parents recalled the episode between themselves, Richard was drifting off into his own thoughts. He was thinking again of the forthcoming funeral.

"You are going to be there on Wednesday aren't you?" he said suddenly, recalling that his mother had told him she was packing.

"Yes, of course," said his father, "we were due to be off on the cruise on Tuesday and that's what we were trying to rearrange earlier today."

"Oh yes, I forgot," said Richard.

His father continued, "We think we can meet the cruise in Hong Kong now at the end of the week rather than at the start of the cruise which is Shanghai. That way we will have a day or so after the funeral to... well, you know."

The table fell silent for a moment as each had their own private thoughts about the funeral.

After what seemed like several minutes, Richard's mother said, "Are you staying in Cambridge tonight dear?"

"Yes, Mum." He looked at the clock and saw it was a little after five p.m. "And I really must be making tracks soon."

They continued to eat, chatting about lighter subjects until Richard decided he needed to go, as the weather report was not good for the evening. He only had a short distance to travel, but it was now dark and bitterly cold and he didn't relish the snow that was threatening, so he left, bidding his parents goodbye. In case he didn't have the opportunity to mention it at the funeral, he reminded them to keep in touch whilst they were away so he knew they were all right. 'How things have changed,' he thought, 'me asking my parents to keep in touch on their travels rather than the other way round.'

From his parents' house Richard walked back to his flat where he prepared a few things, including his black suit and tie and most of what else he needed for the funeral later that week. He looked out the window when he had finished and sure enough, as predicted, the weather had closed in and there was now a dusting of snow lying on the roads and pavements. He moved back to the lounge, turned on the TV and caught the News at Ten before retiring to bed, quite tired and full of the thoughts of the day. That night was not an easy one and Richard found it difficult to sleep for any length of time. By six a.m. on Monday he was wide-awake, but as tired as when he went to bed. Nevertheless, he decided to rise in readiness for work later on in the day. Despite his tiredness, he visited his gym and worked out for an hour or so, then went to a local café for a cappuccino before setting off to work. Monday and Tuesday seemed to pass reasonably quickly as he immersed himself in work. This made him feel positive, as he had not been in for the whole of the previous week. As he worked, it seemed very strange to him not to have his grandfather there by his side giving him the benefit of his extensive wisdom. The fact was, Stuart had hardly been there at all for some time prior to his death, but somehow knowing that he was available to Richard was enough. Sadly, that was no longer true.

On Wednesday, the day of the funeral, Richard had been awake for some time before he heard the sound of his multimedia system radio alarm switching on as the BBC News started. The very first item that he heard was a presenter telling the nation, *'Sir Stuart Harper, the Theoretical Physicist who died recently will be buried today in Oxford following a service at Downing College Chapel at Cambridge University at eleven a.m. The Police have requested that mourners do not cause road blockages on the route from Cambridge to Oxford along which the funeral cortège will travel'*. The presenter paused and then continued with the rest of the news, none of which registered with Richard as he got up, showered and dressed for the funeral. After his third attempt, he had still tied his black tie with the front tail too short. He decided this would not be seen under his dark grey suit jacket and grey overcoat so he did not make a fourth attempt. He couldn't face breakfast, but decided to take himself to the local café again, which was near the University, for a double shot coffee; he felt in need of that. He glanced at himself in the full-length mirror checking his appearance, nodded in approval of the way he looked and left the flat. It was a desperately miserable day, very cold and rain, or more likely, sleet was threatening to fall from the black sky overhead. Just as he reached the café the heavens opened and he regretted not thinking to bring an umbrella. He ordered a cappuccino, paid for it and walked over to a stool at the window bench where he removed and hung up his overcoat and sat holding his coffee mug with both hands to warm them as he stared through the plate glass window at the bleak weather outside. He shivered

and as he did so his mind wandered to the file and its prediction that on the day of his grandfather's funeral he would meet a woman who could teach him about hypnosis. Richard found himself drifting off into a daze, thinking about how hypnosis could possibly fit into the plan, when suddenly, a young woman said, "Is this seat free?" as she pointed at the one next to Richard.
"Wh-what?" said Richard, "P-p-pardon, I mean," he continued after remembering his manners, having been startled by her question.
"Y-yes it is," he continued realising this was a very attractive young woman and the stress they caused him always triggered a slight nervous stutter.
"Thank you" she said as she sat down. "What a positively beastly day."
"Y-yes," Richard said, "it is in-indeed." He put his nose into his coffee cup and took a slow sip not knowing what, if anything, to say next.
"Are you all right?" asked the young lady, "You look as though you're in shock."
"No-no, I, I'm fine," he returned, "Thank-you. I'm, I'm sorry, I, I am miles away, i-it's just that I'm going to a f-f-funeral later, sorry," he continued awkwardly.
"So am I," said the girl, "To Sir Stuart Harper's funeral. Is that where you are going?"
Richard drew breath sharply which was unfortunate as he had just put the coffee cup to his mouth again and he sucked in a mouthful of hot coffee, burning his tongue and the roof of his mouth. Despite this and now choking too he was wondering if this was the girl he was to meet as predicted by his grandfather.
"Y-y-yes, what's your name?" he blurted.

Although slightly bemused by Richard's sudden informality she responded "Helen."
His jaw dropped and his heart missed a beat. 'It's her' he thought.
"Helen Johnston," she added.
"Oh, oh I'm s-s-sorry," he said realising that he had jumped to the wrong conclusion and that his approach had been unseemly. "I, I thought you might have been s-s-someone I am going to m-m-meet at the funeral."
"That's okay," she said with a slightly puzzled look on her face, "actually I am meeting my husband there, he's a researcher at the University".
Richard thought, 'Johnston, Johnston, of course, Alan Johnston one of the researchers at the faculty.' "Is Alan J-J-Johnston your husband?" he said carefully.
"Yes, he is indeed," she replied.
Richard felt foolish and excused himself to go to the toilet. "I-I'm just off; no d-d-doubt I will see you later."
"Yes" she said, "no doubt, good-bye."
"G-good-bye," he said. When Richard came back from the toilet she had left so he sat back down for another ten minutes before leaving too.

Outside the sleet was falling in sheets making the prospect of standing at a graveside about as appealing as an ice bath in winter, almost what it would become. He pulled on his overcoat and left the café with the free newspaper over his head offering scant protection. He covered the few hundred metres to his destination very quickly, darting from refuge to refuge trying to avoid both slush puddles and being completely drenched. When he arrived at the chapel he sought out his family, but when people continually offered condolences he decided to leave them, slid back a few rows and took a seat on his own. He was desperately sad and was not able to converse; he needed to be on his own, at least as much as he could be in the full to overflowing chapel.

To Richard's mind, the service seemed to pass very quickly. He had not attended many such services; he had only been to the cremation of his grandmother and to that of a good friend who had committed suicide due to depression when they were in their mid teens. 'That,' he thought as he recalled it, 'was a particularly harrowing experience'. When his uncle John died a few years back Richard was unable to attend his funeral due to being seriously ill at the time with glandular fever. He had never really got over that, not seeing his favourite uncle off. It was of course unavoidable, due to his illness, but nonetheless upsetting and something of a regret for him. Now however, he felt as though he had come to terms with it. After all, what was it that his grandfather had said in his first posthumous file? 'I am with you, we all are, everyone that has died'. Remembering that gave Richard great comfort, to know that not only was his grandfather with him, so was his beloved uncle John, the man he never really had time to get to know very well, certainly not adult to adult. He smiled at that thought but then realised no one else knew what he knew and if he was seen smiling there, they might think he was being disrespectful, so he bowed his head and waited for the service to end.

5

By the time the cortège reached Oxford, the weather had improved slightly and the sleet had stopped. However it was still very cold and almost everyone was shivering as they stood at the grave's edge.

'It's a strange thing', Richard thought to himself as he looked around at the mourners, 'some of these people seem to know just what to do at such events. They dress appropriately for the weather and correctly for the occasion, walk respectfully, talk compassionately and seem to hold their emotion in check even to the point of being able to sing at the service', something an enormous emotional lump in his throat had prevented him from doing even though he had wanted to. Prior to his knowing about the after-life he felt he could never have spoken at a funeral for fear of cracking up and letting everyone down. Now however, he thought he could handle it and wondered if other people who could too were also perhaps aware of, or at least believed in, an after-life that let them deal with death in such a controlled and calm manner. Then there were the others. Those who were so distraught that they could not think straight, did not put on the correct, or enough, clothes and could not talk at all due to the high level of emotion surging through their bodies making them shake, even on occassion when it was not cold. 'The ones who did not believe in the after-life', he thought. As Richard mused, more words were spoken as the coffin was finally lowered into the family grave. His grandfather's close family threw flowers and some earth into the hole in the ground before turning and leaving the graveside heading towards the cemetery gates to go on to the family's home for the wake. Richard had always thought this to be such an odd custom, leaving the graveside with the person down there on his or her own, but that was before he knew about life after death. Now he knew differently, but he looked back as he walked away from the grave, still choosing to be on his own despite his mother's protestation.

By now Richard had completely forgotten that he was supposed to be making an acquaintanceship with Helen Harrison. Then a young woman who had been walking beside him tripped and started to stumble. Instinctively he caught her, preventing her from falling headlong onto the muddy grass. Clearly she was one of the others he had just been thinking about, as she was completely underdressed for the inclement weather. She was however, appropriately and respectfully dressed in a black skirt suit. Richard looked at her shoes; 'no wonder she tripped', he thought, as one of her high heels had stuck in the mud causing her to miss her footing.

"Thank you she said," gathering her composure.

"N-n-no problem," said Richard, stumbling in his own way, "I'm p-pleased I was there for y-you, that grass doesn't look too, t-too inviting".
"No it doesn't. Thank-you again," said the young woman. "You're Richard Harper aren't you?"
"Y-yes, how do you know?" he replied, as he did not recognise her.
"I used to work with your grandfather sometimes on one of his alternative theories, about the passage of time, he was investigating the passage of time during hypnosis, that's what I do, hypnotherapy. Sorry," she added, "I forgot, you don't know me, my name is Helen Harrison, your grandfather may have mentioned me."

So there it was, he had met Helen Harrison on the day of the funeral just as his grandfather had predicted and the moment had been a lot less distressing than he had expected. Nonetheless, the old stutter had raised its ugly head again, much to Richard's annoyance. Just then the heavens opened again and thick sleet with flakes as large as butterfly wings began to cover them but this time the sleet was much heavier than before. Helen offered to share her umbrella with Richard and he gladly accepted, helping her along the way with his arm around her tiny waist so she didn't trip again. For some reason, despite the close physical contact, he didn't feel the slightest embarrassment, which confused him somewhat. As they walked along entwined under the single umbrella, he was able to observe how elegant she was. He also noticed the aroma of her distinctive perfume which he thought was just wonderful, indeed he thought, 'Helen's wonderful, a very beautiful woman indeed; Grandad didn't mention that'.

The family had arranged numerous cars for family and friends and Helen was invited by Richard to share one of them with him. As they arrived at the wake Helen paid her respects to the family before Richard whisked her away to a quiet corner and very soon they were taking tea and talking to each other about his grandfather. Everyone else was doing that too as they do at the early stages of a wake before moving on to the respectful and sometimes not so respectful party stage that celebrates the life of the person, rather than the death. Richard didn't notice anyone else; he was completely captivated by Helen who by now had cleaned herself up. She had removed the mud from her shoes and legs and had re-applied her makeup. 'She is,' Richard thought, 'truly beautiful.' They whiled the time away talking about everything and nothing and before they knew it people were leaving and they were some of the last to leave. After saying goodbye to the family, Richard's father, who had noticed Richard hadn't let Helen go all afternoon, tactfully told him there was a car free to take him and Helen home; he and Richard's mother and a few close friends would take one of the other arranged cars.

The sleet was not lying because it had warmed up slightly, but nevertheless the trip from Oxford to Helen's house took about two and a half hours. Richard and Helen chatted all the way hardly noticing the severely inclement weather outside. The highly efficient heater in the car was providing a very comfortable environment and they were both far too engrossed in conversation to notice anything until the driver said, "We are here, Sir, Madam".

"Oh, th-thank you," said Richard, unaware that so much time had passed. They had arrived at Helen's house. It appeared to be in a very nice area of Cambridge, but Richard could not make out any detail, as it was dark and the weather made visibility even worse. During the trip Richard had been so intent on finding out about Helen that he had completely forgotten that his grandfather had told him to find out about her specialist area hypnosis and hypnotherapy.
"I, I have r-really enjoyed meeting you today H-Helen. I have had a g-great day."
Realising what he said he continued:
"Oh, that s-sounds awful, after all it's the day of my g-grandfather's funeral, sorry."
'Damn it I'm just no good with words', he thought.
"Don't worry Richard, I know what you mean, I've enjoyed meeting you too even in such sad circumstances, something good comes from everything."
"Thank-thank-you," he said, "may I see you again, perhaps at the weekend?"
"Yes, I would like that very much, but can you do Friday?"
Richard could not believe his luck.
"Y-yes, f-fantastic," he said almost sounding like a turn of the century DJ, "I, I will look f-forward to that."
"Me too," said Helen, kissing him on the cheek as she got out of the limousine, the driver having opened the nearside door.
"Pick me up at eight," she shouted as she skipped up the three stone steps to her front door through the sleet.

'Damn,' he thought, 'I should have seen her to her door, that wasn't very gallant was it?' "Bye." he shouted back as the car drew away to take him to his flat.

Richard felt the next two days until he was able to see Helen again would be agony. He had a knot in his stomach and he knew that Helen was both the cause and the cure. However, slightly relieving his torment just as he was about to get down to work on Thursday, his personal phone bleeped with a text. It was from Helen, and it read, 'Hd grt tme ystrda cant wt 4 2moro'. But how did she get his personal phone number he wondered. He replied 'Helen, it's great to hear from you. I look forward to tomorrow too, see you then, but how did you get my number, I forgot to give it to you, Richard' She laughed when she received his text in proper English and guessed he wasn't comfortable with her abbreviated text language so she telephoned him back. After telling each other again what a great time they had each had meeting the day before she explained that his grandfather had given her Richard's number a few months previously in case of emergency so there was no great mystery. They spoke several more times that day and several more the next and during their sweet nothings agreed that Richard would pick Helen up from her home in Park Terrace. As he walked up the street he noted that the houses were built only on one side and faced a large green open space which he later learned was named Parker's Piece. The houses were on four floors including a basement and were quite magnificent, although many had been turned into student accommodation and required a degree of another sort, a degree of TLC. Richard arrived at the vast solid timber door to Helen's house exactly on time as was evidenced by the bells of the church nearby. He had a large bunch of flowers in his hand that he tried to hide behind his back. As the door opened, he brought the flowers round and said "S-surprise".

"It certainly is, young man," said an attractive middle aged woman, "you must be Richard; come in Helen is nearly ready. I'll find a vase for these beautiful flowers".

Richard was beside himself; the embarrassment of it was almost too much for him as the woman continued, shouting back at him from the kitchen. "She won't be long she's just drying her hair, take a seat in the lounge."

Richard walked into what he assumed to be the lounge and was very pleased when it turned out to be just that; he could not have handled another blunder. Their house was Edwardian and delightfully restored and decorated, if a little dated. The old style box TV in the corner was on and he sat down on the sofa's edge to watch it. He had not seen a cathode ray tube TV like this for years with its curved screen taking up an entire corner of the room. 'How quaint' he thought. At that the lady that he assumed to be Helen's mother came into the room with a vase of flowers in her hands.

"Helen can have these in her room later," she said. "So, young man, I'm Janet, Helen's Mum."

"P-p-pleased to meet you," Richard stammered, still feeling a little embarrassed.

"I hear you work at the University in research." Before he could answer Janet, the door opened and Helen walked in looking absolutely radiant.

"Leave him alone Mum," she said only half jokingly.
"Darling you look beautiful," said Janet.
"Thank–you," replied Helen.
"Anyway," said Janet, "I was only asking Richard about his work."
"Yes I know," said Helen, "the Spanish Inquisition comes in the second sentence. Let's go," she continued, looking towards Richard.
"Before you go, look at the lovely flowers Richard brought for you, Helen."
"Oh thank you, Richard, that was a lovely thought."
Richard smiled at her and blushed, being the shy type. He too wanted to tell Helen how beautiful she looked, but with her mother there that was too much for him.
"I'll put these in your room, Helen."
"Okay, thanks Mum," Helen replied as she walked out in front of them.
As they left the room there were the usual final words of a mother that Richard knew quite well too. "Don't be late darling".
Helen said to Richard in the hall outside the lounge, "She only said that to try to embarrass me, more than in any sense expecting me to do anything other than what I have always done, exactly as I please. She'll apologise later after she's thought it through and realises that it was probably more to do with her own embarrassment about me bringing home a man than anything else. I've never done that before."
Helen, feeling for a few moments in her cavernous handbag for keys, realised she had left them in her room.
"Just a moment, Richard, I've left my keys upstairs," and she left Richard in the hallway.

From the hall, Richard heard a man's voice in the lounge, Helen's father he assumed, who must have come in through the dining room and into the adjoining lounge from the garden. The door was not completely closed and he heard Janet say, "Oh Jim, you have just missed them, Helen looked beautiful."
"That's a shame," he said, "I would have liked to have seen the new man".
"Oh, I don't think he would have coped with two of us," said Janet, "he's a bit shy."
"Is he?" Jim laughed. "Just like me then."
Richard could see through the slight gap between the door and the jamb that Jim kissed his wife on the cheek and pulled her close to him by her waist. At that they both laughed and settled down to the TV just as Helen came down the stairs, opened the front door and almost dragged Richard out with her before he could say anything. Outside, Richard told Helen what he had heard and seen. Helen told Richard that she was thankful he had not had to suffer more embarrassment as her dad had a wicked sense of satire and Richard didn't need that on a first date.

They walked round the corner to one of Richard's favourite restaurants, The Cow, a cross between traditional and contemporary with its airy and spacious rooms with laminate flooring and some exposed brickwork. During their meal they sat in one of the old church pews next to each other rather than opposite. They were completely absorbed by each other's company to the exclusion of all the bustle around them in this popular venue. After their meal they retired to one of the comfortable leather sofas upstairs for a few drinks, still oblivious to the world at large.

Eventually, they left The Cow and sauntered the short distance back to Helen's house still completely immersed in a world of their own and unaware of the cold weather. During their evening they had covered almost every subject imaginable including what each other did and Helen's hypnotherapy work. Richard showed great interest in her work and that pleased her enormously as some of her previous male friends had been less than complimentary about her chosen career. She agreed to show him her studio where she practiced her specialism, saying he should come there over the weekend. Richard was delighted by this as he felt sure that she would be able to give him the information he needed before he listened to more of his grandfather's file. Additionally of course, he found Helen stunning and couldn't wait to see her again irrespective of his need to learn. She too seemed to be very attracted to him and that was rather unusual for Richard as he normally found it difficult to communicate with women in a way that they found interesting. Helen however was different, as it all seemed so natural and easy with her, at least compared to his previous attempts to be with a woman.

As they reached the front door of her house Helen said "Good, it looks as though they're in bed."
"Wh-who, your p-parents?" Richard said hoping he was right, convinced that meeting her father was not a good idea after a drink or few and that it could wait for another time.

"Yes." she said as she climbed the few steps to the magnificent front door of her parent's house. As they stood on the top step Richard shuffled trying to find the right words to say goodnight, not knowing if he should kiss her. As he thought this, Helen acted. She threw her arms round Richard's muscular shoulders and planted a kiss firmly on his lips.
"Thank you for a lovely evening," she said. Richard could feel the blood rushing to his cheeks but it was dark so Helen would not have noticed.
"I, I enjoyed it t-too," he said, wrapping his arms round her shapely figure. They kissed again before Helen opened the door and left Richard after first agreeing to see him again on Sunday when she said she would tell him more about hypnosis. Richard was ecstatic, he had enjoyed a fantastic evening and hardly noticed the light snow beginning to fall as he ambled his way home, scuffing the soles of his shoes on the pavement as he walked, kicking an imaginary stone. He was indeed pleased with himself.

Because he was seeing Helen on Sunday he didn't make his usual trip to St John's Wood and so on Saturday he went to his Cambridge Club to train and filled his day with that, shopping for toiletries, food and other mundane and ordinary activities to while the time away. He even managed to catch up with his oldest and best friend, Bill, or "Bunter" as Richard called him. He had been named that as a result of the rather portly physique he had when he was younger. Now however he would be considered to have an excellent physique, not unlike Richard himself in fact. They whiled away a few hours together although Richard was rather cool when Bunter enquired about his work, or indeed Helen. He kept that quiet too, he didn't need Bunter's wicked ribbing. The day was interspersed with calls from and to Helen, the content of which were crammed with sweet nothings in both directions, but not when Bunter was around. Richard was thankful for that as he would have been merciless in his mockery, 'Richard with a girl,' Bunter would have said, 'I've never heard of such a thing.' All in all it was an interesting day of reflection for Richard who was greatly looking forward to the following day when he would go to Helen's studio.

6

On Sunday, as usual it was the early morning campanologists that were Richard's alarm clock. As always, he thought of his parents and smiled before getting up. He was going to meet Helen, so after more than the normal ablutions, he started to think about what he was going to wear. He tried on several combinations, none of which seemed to fit the bill before finally deciding to wear his brown cords, brown brogues, and a blue cotton shirt with a white T-shirt underneath. This was pretty much what he wore every day, but what could he do? He knew his dress sense was somewhat wanting and by now Helen also knew that. He figured that if he was at least clean, as he always was, he ought to get away with it. Taking a look in the mirror as he completed his outfit, he smiled, pleased with himself, grabbed his long raincoat and left the flat to head towards Helen's studio. He had offered to collect her from home, but she had wanted to arrive before him to prepare the studio before he arrived.

After a short walk, Richard found the studio in a little white painted brick cottage property in a small mews built to the rear of some large period houses. In

Brookside there were a number of such small buildings, some of which were used as homes, others as offices and a few more were used as studios. It was a good mix as it meant that parking was never an issue with the different uses having different needs in terms of timing. That however did not concern Richard as he had walked. He approached the slender slatted door along the narrow street and reached for the doorbell just as Helen opened the door.

"G-goodness, are you ps-s-sychic too?" He exclaimed.

Helen laughed and showed him the milk bottle she had in her hand.

"Come in," she said laughing and placing the bottle on the doorstep, letting Richard pass by her. It was a tight squeeze but neither minded that.

He climbed the narrow stairs to the first floor and turned to see Helen behind him.

"Take off your coat and make yourself comfortable," she said, reaching out to help him off with the coat. Richard slipped the raincoat off and Helen hung it up.

"Your jacket," she continued.

"Y-yes," he replied thinking that an odd comment, but assuming she didn't like it.

"No you idiot, take that off too, it's rather warm in here with the fire."

Richard, feeling such a fool and realising what she had meant, slipped off his jacket which she also hung up. He looked across the room to see a raging log fire and candles burning everywhere. He thought Helen must have got there quite early to have set all this up. Turning to her he complimented her about the ambience of the studio and then remembered to do the same for the way she looked. She smiled and she kissed him, making him feel even warmer than the fire did.

Helen offered him a drink and when he asked for coffee she said she didn't have coffee there, explaining she had found that it could interfere with the hypnosis. He opted for iced sparkling water and Helen joined him in that. Taking their drinks they both settled on the floor next to the fire and started to discuss the Saturday each of them had had. Richard told Helen that his had been pretty boring in that he had only done the usual, mundane Saturday type things, but Helen already knew that as they had been on the phone to each other several times in the day. He also told her about meeting Bunter. Helen was not impressed by the nickname, suggesting it was cruel. Better that Richard should call him by his proper name William, or even Bill but not Bunter. She asked him not to call him that in front of her when she finally met him. He agreed but only after complaining that Bunter would most likely continue to call him Dick, which he hated. He didn't tell her that though mainly because sometimes he knew he could be one. Helen looked at him and the look was one Richard now recognised as, 'I rest my case'.
Helen's day had been more interesting in that she had something to show for her efforts. She had been shopping and in fact the outfit she had on was one she had bought earlier. Richard was appreciative again and complimented her on how well the short dress fitted her, blushing as he did so. Helen smiled, she loved the way Richard was so shy, but didn't comment as she was conscious that he would be even more embarrassed that she loved it.

"So Richard, you want to know about hypnosis?"
"Y-yes, v-very much."
"I take it that you have never been hypnotised then."
"No, no actually, I have n-not," he said, realising where this was possibly leading.
"Well, let me explain what hypnosis does and how it works first, then perhaps I can hypnotise you."
He was right, it was leading where he though it was going to.
"We, we will s-see," he said hesitantly.
"It will assist you to understand what it's all about," she said reassuringly, but firmly, "but it's up to you, if you don't want to that's fine; but remember, anything you do under hypnosis will be your decision. I can't make you do anything that your subconscious doesn't want you to do."
"R-really? H-how does that work?"
"Well," she continued, "have you seen anyone being hypnotised on stage before?"
"Y-yes."
"They often act the fool or react to a command or noise that triggers a particular movement or set of movements," said Helen. "For instance, a handclap may result in the hypnotised person neighing like a donkey. The reason they do that is that their subconscious is willing to let them do it. If it were not, they quite simply would not react."
Richard interjected, thinking of his own personality, "B-but sometimes these people are very quiet and r-reserved. Why would they allow themselves to w-w-willingly become a figure of fun?"
"For that very reason, deep down, they may want to be less stuffy or rigid in their self control or even be

desperate to be the centre of attention and their normal self will not allow them to be."
"Is it not d-dangerous?"
"No, not at all. These people are in full control and their subconscious will still impose a limit on what they are prepared to do. However, whilst it can be very entertaining it is not very scientific and I don't become involved in such showmanship. I prefer to assist people to overcome fears, phobias and ailments using hypnotherapy and this is where it all happens." She gestured to the surroundings of the room. Apart from the fire, the candles on some low tables and on the fire hearth, a rug in front of the hearth and a few colour block paintings on the walls there was little in the way of furnishing except a reclining leather chair with a blanket on it and a matching leather upright wing back chair.

Helen beckoned towards the reclining chair and Richard stood up and moved towards it then stopped.
"Are you s-s-sure about this?" he asked, looking more than slightly worried.
"Perfectly," she replied, standing up herself and coming over all serious, a side that Richard had not seen to date. He was slightly reassured by her look as he sat down, moving the blanket aside as he did so.
"O-okay," he stammered.
As he sat there waiting for Helen to do or say something he suddenly realised that he was gripping the arms of the chair very tightly. He was very nervous and with his limited understanding of hypnosis he felt he was about to give up his control to Helen. This scared him all the more because he was by now very sure he was in love

with her and desperately did not want to make a fool of himself. He relaxed his grip and moved to try to get comfortable. Just as he did so Helen pulled a lever on the outside of the arm of the chair and it reclined with a start that caused Richard to jump.
"It's okay." Helen said reassuringly, as Richard half smiled, half winced, but tried to relax his grip again. Richard watched Helen as she moved to the upright chair and sat down. She very quickly made herself comfortable and still. Richard thought she looked very self-assured. She looked up at Richard to see him still squirming and said, "Richard, if at any time during your hypnotic state you feel uncomfortable with what is happening to you, you can stop. Simply discontinue listening to me and open your eyes and you will return to your normal fully awake self." Richard smiled awkwardly and said in a weak voice "Okay H-Helen," as he crossed his legs.

Helen started by telling Richard to find a comfortable position, close his eyes and to relax with his legs uncrossed as she got up and placed the blanket over his lower-half, also telling him that it was so that he would not feel cold during his hypnotic state. Helen settled herself back into her chair and relaxed before starting to talk, pausing for a few moments before commencing.
"Are you comfortable, Richard?"
"Y-yes thank-you," he replied, feeling quite out of his control zone.
"Then we shall begin," Helen said, somewhat like a child's storyteller.

"Richard, ….. I want you now to take a deep breath, hold it for a moment and then breathe out slowly and, as you do so, allow your entire body to relax."
Richard breathed in, held if for a couple of seconds and exhaled slowly as he had been instructed. Helen continued, "I want you to concentrate on your breathing, do it slowly, evenly and deliberately ... be aware of your breathing as you relax and as I speak. From time to time, you may be aware of some sounds or noises from the building or from outside. These won't disturb you, indeed, they will assist you to relax further, the only sound you are interested in is my voice. I want you to relax fully, make yourself completely at ease and close your eyes. That's it, be completely at ease and relaxed, close your eyes… Permit your mind to be free, free and to drift anywhere it cares to go, anywhere your mind would feel safe for you to be… and, be aware of your muscles, allow them to go limp and loose, your feet and ankles want to relax, let them relax, that's it, let them relax, ... to become limp. Allow your calves to go too, let them be loose and fully relaxed, your knees and thighs, let your thighs relax, allow them to be loose too, that's it."
As she was speaking, Richard thought how different Helen's voice had become; she was speaking with an encouraging tone and without hesitation but with planned pauses between suggestions that he felt compelled to follow. She continued, "You can now feel a heaviness in your legs, they are beginning to feel very heavy, very heavy indeed. Let them be as heavy as lead and as that happens you are starting to feel lethargic, very happy and rested… now, that feeling is spreading

upwards to your abdominal muscles, let those muscles fully relax, ... really enjoy the feeling."
Helen continued to give instructions to Richard telling him to relax fully every part of his body from foot to head, telling him that he should go down deeper and deeper into a relaxed state and let his body feel drowsier and drowsier, to relax completely.

After ten minutes or so coaxing Richard to relax she said, "As you relax in a deep and comfortable state, you are breathing freely and easily and the sound of my voice will continue to help you to relax ever more deeply. You are secure in the thought that there is nothing for you to do except relax, nobody wanting anything, nothing at all that you need to do... Simply listen to my voice." She paused for a short while and then continued in the same calm voice as before. "In a few moment's time you will hear me say the word..." She paused again for several seconds and then said the word, "now" but in such a way that she made it sound like a command. What Richard actually heard Helen say was the word 'now' but it was on the back of a long exhalation in the way of a long sigh. He also noticed that she appeared to have timed saying this word to coincide precisely with the exhalation of his own breath.
"And whenever you hear me say the word 'noooowwwwww' every muscle of your body from the top of your head to the tip of your toes is further relaxing, any nervous tension will disapear from your body and your body will continue to sink down more and be looser and looser, more relaxed and comfortable. Your body is going to relax more and

more. You will be entirely at peace. You will also be aware of a very pleasant feeling through your whole body."
Richard by now was noticing that he was indeed feeling very relaxed and any feeling of anxiety that existed earlier had completely disapeared. He did not however feel as though he was hypnotised, 'whatever that is' he thought, but continued in any event as he was actually enjoying the feeling.

As he drifted in and out of thought Helen continued, "And, ... noooowwwwww you can begin to pay closer attention to the words I say, becoming even more at ease, you will happily enter into an ever deepening concentration which can and will take you deeper and deeper as we go on."
Helen paused again briefly before saying, "And noooowwwwww I would like you to imagine you are standing on a landing at the top of a long flight of stairs, you don't need to know yet where they lead, only that you are completely safe as they are strong stairs, well lit and wide. Soon, I will count down from 10 to 1 to help you relax even more deeply and you will also walk down the stairs in your own time, it is very safe and you are in control of the time it will take you to descend. You may find yourself with a curious sense of excitement with each step and when you step off at the bottom, when you have descended all the steps and completely at your own pace, you will find yourself in your private control room, this is the control room of your mind, where you go when you dream and the control room is different for everybody."

She continued to describe what the control room might look like, saying for some it was a large place like a huge control room in a power station and for others it was more compact, perhaps similar to a recording studio. She told him that how he perceived the room did not matter, all that did matter was he understood that he could change settings there to alter how he reacted to situations in his life, to reduce stress, to relax more, to assist concentration, to overcome phobias, to assist in curing ailments.

She carried on, telling him that was how he dealt with problems naturally when he slept. Also, that it was natural and that his mind was finding a way of solving a problem, looking for different ways of dealing with issues, helping him to let go of any unnecessary nervous tension associated with that problem. Helping him to reconnect with an appropriate way of dealing with that problem and responding appropriately. The next time he came into contact with the old problem he would find himself responding differently, appropriately and the first time this happened he might be surprised, but he would soon forget that he was responding in a new way because it would just feel so right. She started counting to take him down the stairs and deeper into hypnosis. "10, ... 9, and another step down." As she said 'down', it was in a similar manner to the word 'now' and again matched with his breathing pattern, "8, ... 7, ... 6, slowly, leisurely, at your own pace ... 5, ... 4, ... 3, and doooowwwnnnn another step, another step doooowwwnnnn 2, 1 and rest. Can you see a door? ... Open that door and step into your control room and begin to explore the room. Review everything that's there, take your time and be aware of what is there."

Richard came off the stairs to a solid light ash door. It had a chrome lever handle on the left and a key in the lock below. In a somewhat surreal way he watched his right hand move to the key, which he turned anti-clockwise and then to the lever, which he depressed to open the door. It swung back out of his way giving him free acccess to a room beyond. He could see racks of slide switches and he could feel his mind wandering towards them thinking about what the various switches could do. From a distance he thought he could read panels headed emotions, fitness, intellect, health and one that read stress. As he explored his own control room that resembled, not surprisingly, a chemist's laboratory, Helen said "I would like you to 'noooowwwwww' slowly and carefully move towards that control you have selected. Relax and notice that your breathing has slowed down. You are completely relaxed and at ease with yourself. Now you can move towards the control panel and study it properly. See the particular switch that has caught your attention, study that too. The switch has something written on it and you can see that it is turned up way too high. If you would like to do so ..... noooowwwwww slide the knob a little, and only a little, so you reduce your sensitivity to what it is that worries you."

Richard had chosen the 'stress' panel and in particular a small sliding switch labelled 'speech'. He had always had a bit of a stutter when he was nervous, particularly in front of girls and his mind had directed him to that control. In his mind he slid the knob vertically downwards noticing that it was finely ratcheted. He slid it over the ratchets, notch by notch.

Helen continued her monologue, "That's it, reduce the level slightly. After that you can get used to responding in a new and less agitated way and afterwards, as you sleep and dream, your mind will reduce your sensitivity to the issue you have chosen to deal with, ... and how you feel about the new way in which you deal with your issue, to the point where it will feel completely natural to you and, in time, you will look back and wonder what all the fuss was about."
The practical side of the hypnosis now completed, Helen spent a few more moments reinforcing the idea she had implanted before moving to the process of waking him from his hypnotic state.

She then started to give Richard instructions to leave the control room and to close the door behind him, lock it and place the key somewhere where he could find it easily if he needed to return there. Her voice started to speed up and become more authoritative, "move to the stairs, climb them quickly but safely." She spoke in an ever more controlling voice and louder, "You may notice your heart beating a little faster. When you reach the top you can begin to refocus on the here and now. In a few moments I am going to bring you to a full waking alert state. Every part of you will be back in the here and now feeling completely normal with all sensations returned to you and fully functioning. You will hear me count from 1 to 10. By the count of 8 your eyes will naturally, easily, open and by the count of 10 you will be fully awake. Your normal sensations will be returned, you will feel good, very refreshed, refocused and as the days, weeks and months go by you notice more and more the changes taking place; small changes at first, but from the future when you look back you can know how far you have come, so ready 1, 2, 3 more aware 4, 5, 6 more alert, 7, 8 eyes fully open 9, 10 fully awake."

She stopped talking and sat silently looking at Richard. He was now sitting in the reclining chair looking thoroughly relaxed, but as though he had just woken up to this world from another, slightly dazed and more than a little amazed and bemused at what he had just experienced. He sat forward and was about to talk when he suddenly remembered what he had thought about when he was hypnotised, if that was what had happened to him. He tried to speak, but was dumbstruck, unable to recall how to engage in conversation with his mind in overdrive thinking about what had just happened, it was all he could do to raise a faint smile for Helen. Clearly well used to this response, she got up from her chair and moved to the rug in front of the fire beckoning him to join her there. Richard, in one movement, found the recline lever, pulled it, kicked the footrest back and rolled forward to restore the chair to the normal sitting position. He picked up the fallen blanket she had draped over him at the start of the session, folded it and placed it carefully on the arm of the chair as he got up. He felt surprisingly refreshed as he sat down on the floor next to Helen on the rug.

Helen asked Richard how he felt during the hypnosis. Now, he was able to speak and he told her that he was not sure he had been hypnotised as his thoughts had at times been distracted away from her voice.
"Oh, you were definitely hypnotised," said Helen, "all the usual signs were present."
"What signs?" asked Richard inquisitively.
"Well," she continued, "you were swallowing a lot in the early stages that showed me that you were entering hypnosis. Also, your breathing was very much reduced in rate and you were sighing a lot, all clear signs of a state of hypnosis, the rate of breathing tells me the depth of your hypnotic state"
"Gosh." he said. "I have no recollection of that but what about me drifting off your voice to my own thoughts during the session?"
"That's normal," explained Helen, "so long as you come back to my voice you will continue to be hypnotised. You were definitely hypnotised, and I can convince you very easily."
"How?" asked Richard.
"Without looking at your watch, how long do you think the session lasted?"
Richard hadn't expected such a simple question and he looked around for a clock but there wasn't one.
"About twenty minutes?" he offered, more as a question than as an answer.
Helen smiled, "You're nearly right," she said, teasing him, "it was actually just over an hour." "You're kidding me," replied Richard shocked; but upon checking his watch he realised she was not. "That's amazing," he continued, "I was convinced it was not a very long time."

“Almost everyone who is actually hypnotised underestimates how long a session has lasted,” said Helen, “and usually by about a margin of error similar to yours in the early sessions, although it does vary with the depth of hypnosis. If you were in a very deep state a session of an hour can appear to have taken only a few minutes.”
“What do you mean ‘everyone who is actually hypnotised’ are some people not then?” asked Richard.
“Yes,” said Helen, “some people cannot be successfully hypnotised.”
“Have you ever been hypnotised Helen?” he asked.
“Oh yes,” she replied, “often, and I self hypnotise also to relax and prepare myself for major events and meetings.”
“Really, how do you do that?” asked Richard.
“By using a recording of another hypnotherapist,” she replied.
Richard continued probing, “But how do you come out of it?”
“The recording will ask me to come out of it or my brain just tells me it’s time to wake up if I have dropped off to sleep during the session. There is no magic to this Richard, you will realise as you learn more, if you want to that is.”
“Yes please,” he responded with enthusiasm, “it’s fascinating, and I can see why my grandfather was so interested.”
“Yes, he was a firm believer in it,” said Helen, “and,” she continued, “dare I say it, have you noticed that your stutter has disappeared?”
Richard, stopped to think about what he had been saying and was astounded to realise that his stutter had

indeed vanished. They continued to chat for a while longer before Richard ceased to think about what had just happened to him and again realised he was in the company of one of the most beautiful women he had ever known. Sitting as they were on the floor in front of the fire on a rug, they were quite close to each other when all of a sudden Richard caught the aroma of Helen's perfume. It had been there all the time of course, but he hadn't noticed it until then. He gently sniffed the air, slightly raising his head as he did so. "Mmm," he said, "your perfume is wonderful."

"Thank you Richard," Helen said, moving closer to him as she said it. Richard suddenly realised what he had said and felt embarrassed. This was not the way he normally acted, he looked away towards the fire. Helen realising his anguish put her hand on his cheek and guided his face towards her own and said to him "Richard, I'm here."

He looked straight into her stunning blue eyes that seemed to be hypnotising him again. She moved even closer and embraced him planting a kiss firmly on his lips. Richard responded equally, managing to overcome his shyness. He wasn't stammering but that was because they weren't talking now as they entwined and spent the next hour or so getting to know each other rather better than they had to date.

7

Almost two months had passed since Stuart had died and as the old man had suggested, Richard had been busy learning as much as he could about hypnosis and hypnotherapy. Helen, Richard's now almost daily companion, had taught him everything he felt he needed to know before going back to listen to the second recording. It was a Saturday and he had travelled the previous night back to his St John's Wood apartment for the first time since meeting Helen. He had already sent a copy of his grandfather's file ahead via email as a further back up, so on his arrival at the London flat he found himself eager to get on with it and approached the multimedia system and commanded, "System on". The lights on the wall burst into life and there was a gentle hum as the system waited patiently for the next command. Richard used the remote control computer panel to select the file and hit 'Play' unsure of what was to come.

"Hello Richard", said the digital voice immediately, "I trust you are well."
"Yes thank-you, very well but then you knew that," Richard said in a rather cheeky retort.

“Yes I did, but,” said his grandfather “being polite is very important where I am now and I suppose it’s starting to rub off on me. I could be very rude in my past life, ignoring people, sometimes people who dearly cared for me. That was due to my perception of a lack of time, but that is no longer the case and soon it will not be a problem for you either. You remember what I told you the last time we spoke?”
“Yes, that there is an after-life and I am talking to someone who is from it.”
“No, not that bit, the part that will affect you during your lifetime and that of everyone else on the planet. I told you that we use only part of our brain power and that we have the capacity to live much longer than we do, both of which shortcomings can be changed and I have the knowledge to pass on to you. I also asked you to go and learn about hypnotism and its use in hypnotherapy. The reason is that this is the key to accessing your greater brain power and ultimately to longer life, and this you did well. I have been following your progress with Helen.”
“What, all of it?” exclaimed Richard, “Including my time with Helen?” He almost squealed out.
“Yes, all of it,” came the reply.
“Gross!” commented Richard in a somewhat juvenile outburst that he was apt to indulge in from time to time.
His grandfather laughed. “I’m afraid you will have to get used to that idea from now on my boy, but you don’t need to tell anyone else just yet,” his grandfather both teased and warned.

As his grandfather continued, Richard became more and more captivated. Here he was about to learn the secrets of ultimate brainpower and vastly increased life from a man who had died two months earlier.

"Why me, why me, Grandad?"

"Even before I died, I knew you would be curious enough to check my computer for any unfinished work that may have been there so you could take it over. You are the only person who had my passwords so therefore, you were the obvious choice. Also, you are young enough to benefit from all of this and to see the process through for the next hundred years or so."

Whilst still astonished by all that was going on, Richard seemed content at this answer and was already considering the task of being the driver of the change of humanity.

After allowing Richard a moment or two to absorb his answer, his grandfather continued. "To date, hypnosis has only been used to excite and titillate at worst and to treat minor addiction and phobias at best. However, I have learned that hypnosis is the key to all of what I have told you is possible and that is why you needed to get up to speed on the subject. You will also need the assistance of Helen in this and she will give it willingly."

"So I need to tell Helen about all of this now and bring her along to hear this first hand?" questioned Richard.

"No, not yet," said his grandfather. "There's plenty of time for that and I want you to fully understand the implications of the responsibility, for it is just that, a responsibility, and a mighty big one. And, it must appear to be your idea for now."

"Okay," said Richard, nodding, but that brings me to another question. You have answered why me, but why you?"

"That's easy. Scientists have, as you know, been trying to communicate with the dead for hundreds of years. Recently skullcaps with electrodes, similar to the one I wore to communicate with my computer, have been used to monitor brain function at and after death. However, these have been placed on people just before death so the brain function did not have time to adjust to the cap. I wore mine twenty-four hours a day for many years, it became part of me and thus I was able to 'talk', for the want of a better word, through it with ease. In fact the recordings that you have were made in only a fraction of a second after my death but the computer 'speaks the words' at normal speed so the recording times are as you found them. It was still a communication after death but only just after, as we lose the ability to communicate with your stage of life shortly after death. Thus my 11 hours of recording is the only communication I can or will have with you or indeed anyone else; so you see Richard, if you do not agree it may be a long time before this opportunity arises again. Why me?" he said returning to his grandson's earlier question, "I had no choice in the matter, it was destined."
"Are you telling me that all of what we do in life is fate?" exclaimed Richard.
"Yes, to a great extent," said his grandfather, "although there are exceptions."
"To what extent and what exceptions?" asked Richard demandingly.

"Well, you are the one chosen to pass on this invaluable knowledge."
"And the exceptions?" Richard said butting in impatiently.
"The exception is not in your control, it is in mine," said his grandfather. "The future is set. If you decide not to do this for humanity, you may not and events from now on may be such that you pass the files on to someone else with whom I can communicate in the same way as I do with you. However, if you decide to proceed, we will continue. Either way, your decision is fate and I know the outcome so that is the exception. I know all, you are free to make your decision, but it will not really be a decision, it will be providence."

Richard sat back and reflected. He was about to make the greatest decision of his life, but it was one that was already made. Whatever his decision, he could not, he was being told, alter the outcome. However after a few moments reflection, this was, he supposed, exactly what he was used to as a scientist. He was open to any conclusion, but he could not influence it, what transpired in a experiment could not be changed, the result was pre-determined, much in the way of his grandfather's proposal. Similar to an experiment, he could either do it or not, but if he didn't, he could guarantee that someone would at some time or another.
"One question?" Richard said.
Not waiting for the answer, his grandfather interrupted, "Who is the one the file will pass to if you refuse to do this deed?"

"Yes," Richard said slowly, a bit bemused that his grandfather had correctly predicted his question, although he didn't know why he felt like that.

"Whom do you suppose?" asked his grandfather?

"I don't know," Richard replied, now slightly irritated by this conversation.

"Helen Harrison," came the answer.

"What, my Helen?" Richard was flabbergasted. The girl he had come to know so well over the past two months was the alternative bearer of the information that would change the world if he refused. He realised that he had no choice to make, either way he would be involved and in the second instance if he refused, Helen might see him as a feeble individual and not want him. Suddenly he realised something and thought, 'What am I thinking? Here I am on the edge of a discovery that will make me world famous and I am considering not doing it. I will do it, not just for Helen, but for the sake of science, I must continue fate or no fate.'

"Okay, Grandad, I will do it," Richard blurted out, "but then you knew that didn't you?"

"Yes," his grandfather replied, "Yes I did."

"Goodness," Richard continued, "now I know how Moses must have felt taking the tablets from God to pass on the commandments to the world."

"Richard, I am not God in anyone's terms, but yes, you are the chosen messenger to the world and thus you may consider yourself as a Moses. However for the time being the concepts and ideas that I am going to pass to you will be seen as your own. It must be that way initially, as the people will not be ready for the full truth until their intelligence quota has been increased."

Fear of the unknown was not usually an issue for Richard but in this case he was scared. He was about to ask his grandfather more about what he would face when his grandfather said he could not continue further, as the doorbell was about to ring. Sure enough, the bell rang a few seconds later and Richard asked his grandfather who it was. "It's Helen of course, you said you would see her today, it's her birthday, she's twenty-eight, she's come to London especially to meet you, you haven't forgotten have you? Go on my boy, take her out, spoil her and have fun, we can come back to this when you have time."

"I had forgotten. Your file seems to take all of my thoughts just recently. Okay I will take her out now, but only if you promise not to watch us."

His grandfather laughed as Richard said "System to TV" and the TV switched on as he went to the door to let Helen in.

Richard gathered his thoughts as he opened the door to the flat.

"Hi, Helen."

Richard greeted Helen with a hug. Helen responded hugging him too and kissing him on the lips as they both stood on the doorstep.

"Ooh" she said, "that was nice, I hope there's more of that later."

Richard blushed; he still hadn't got the hang of this emotion thing.

"Aren't you going to ask me in, Richard, it's pretty cold out here?" she said playing on his shyness and loving every minute of it.

"Yes of course, come in and happy birthday. I've got a lovely day planned," said Richard, regaining his composure.
"Thank you, I can't wait," she said with a twinkle in her eye. Helen of course had mastered the art of people skills as her job demanded and she was very artful at teasing Richard, but not in a mean way, she just liked to be playful. She could be quite serious too though, and dominant as she needed to be when hypnotising someone. She was in a long dark blue overcoat with a red scarf, dressed for the cold winter day that it was. Underneath she had a pretty, pale blue, short skirt with colour matched soft cashmere jumper that showed off her beautiful figure perfectly and long knee length black boots.
"Where are we going? Am I dressed for it?" she asked.
"Perfect," he said "just the ticket."
'God' he thought, 'what a stupid thing to say'.

As for him, he was a mess, unshaven and he had just dragged on joggers when he got up; but she didn't mind, she liked the transformation that could take place and she watched the news on TV whilst Richard got ready, which took precisely ten minutes. While he was doing that he had called Brown's Restaurant in London from the bathroom on his mobile phone to book a table. He returned to Helen to hear her approval of the way he looked as she straightened his collar. They were off to the first birthday destination, which was almost as much a surprise to Richard as it was to Helen. Fortunately he had partly planned ahead and at least had her present and a card in his jacket pocket. So he was winging it and prayed that the food and service at

Brown's, a place he knew well from his University days in Oxford, would be similar in London.

Arriving at the restaurant they were greeted at the door and no one let slip that the reservation had just been made. They sat at the bar initially and had a drink whilst waiting for their table to be set. When it was ready, a waitress took them to a window table. Richard smiled at the thought of his grandfather watching over him as he wondered if it was he who got them the best table in the house. He smiled again with pleasure as he watched Helen, hearing her squeal with delight. After five minutes at the table, Richard excused himself telling Helen that he needed to go to the men's room. He went to the rear of the restaurant and as he got there he noticed that the fire door was open. Opposite, there was a bucket shop for theatre tickets and there was no queue. He darted over to the little shop and bought two tickets for that evening to see Chicago at London's Cambridge Theatre. He could not believe his luck and then he remembered that it wasn't luck it was his fate as his grandfather had told him. Either way he was pleased with the outcome. As he got back into Brown's through the rear door he nearly forgot to go to the toilet in his excitement to get back to Helen.

A minute later and he was nonchalantly walking back to the table where Helen was patiently waiting. He kissed her on the cheek as he sat down.
"You were a long time," she said.
"Oh there was a queue" he replied trying not to look her in the eye by burying his head in the menu.

"What, in the Gent's?" she said in disbelief.
"Er, the cleaner was in at first." he continued. He hated lying but this was absolutely necessary at this point; perhaps he would tell her later, or perhaps not, he thought.
"Have you chosen what you want?" he said trying to change the subject.
"Nearly," she said, "I was waiting for you."
They both returned to their menus for a minute or two to choose their food and drinks without speaking. They then consulted each other on their choices and found they had both made the same selection. They laughed as they realised and Richard thought of his parents who often did this when they dined out. Now having the same tastes seemed to be becoming a habit for him and Helen, as this was not the first time it had happened.

The Champagne arrived first of all and the waiter poured two glasses. Richard raised his flute and said:
"Happy birthday Helen, cheers."
She lifted her glass and clinked it against his replying "Thank you Richard, cheers."
He reached into his inside pocket and pulled out a pink envelope handing it to Helen with a wry smile.
"Thank you," she said again, opening the envelope. Inside there was a card with a fluffy kitten on the front. Richard had been unsure of whether to buy a joke card or a romantic one, but when he heard Helen say in a childlike voice "Aw look at the little kitten." he knew that he had gone down the right route. Inside the card, Richard had written 'To Helen, on the first birthday we have shared together, may there be many more, with all my love Richard'.

"How lovely, Richard," she said leaning over to kiss him in thanks. As she did so he again reached into his pocket and placed a small cube-like, beautifully wrapped and bowed present on the table.

Suddenly, he realised this could be mistaken for a ring box and panicking as he sincerely hoped that Helen would not think it was a ring and then be disappointed; or perhaps she would be afraid that it was a ring at such an early stage of their relationship. Confusion could have been his middle name at this point as he said: "This is for you too Helen. It's not a ring in case you were thinking..."

"No," said Helen putting him out of his clear misery as she looked neither relieved nor disappointed, "I didn't think that, but that would be nice too." Now he was really confused, was she saying she wanted a ring? Or was she just saying that to make him feel better? He was at a total loss and deciding to move on, he said, "Go on then, open it."

She smiled and picked up the small box pulling the ribbon off with ease. She peeled back the wrapping paper to reveal a small, blue jeweller's box that could indeed have been mistaken for a ring box. However, inside was a pair of white gold set, light blue opal earrings with a tiny card that read 'The colour of the blue of these earrings reminded me of your eyes, but the earrings are not nearly as stunning'. Helen by now had a tear in one of her beautiful eyes and as she wiped it away she moved across to Richard once again and hugged him for what seemed to Richard a very long time.

"Thank you she said, thank you, they are beautiful and just what I wanted."

He was ever so slightly embarrassed by her open show of emotion at such an exposed table in the restaurant, but did his best to overcome it for the sake of the moment.
"Put them on," he suggested.
She did and sure enough they did complement her eyes perfectly and she admired them in a vanity mirror taken from her handbag, smiling as she did so.

A girl at the adjacent table who had been watching all of this closely looked across and said:
"They're beautiful and really suit you; you're lucky to have such a thoughtful boyfriend."
As she spoke, she gave her own boyfriend a dig in the ribs with her elbow as if to say, 'You never do anything like that for me'. Her boyfriend looked surprised. Richard on the other hand was very pleased with himself and oblivious to it all, he had only Helen on his mind and cared not for the thoughts or problems of others at that time. Just at that point their starters arrived at their table.

After the meal, which neither of them really noticed, being so infatuated with each other, they spent the remainder of the afternoon strolling around London's sightseeing attractions. The weather was kind to them for March as it was cold, but dry and they both were dressed for the worst. It gave Helen an excuse, if she needed one, to get even closer to Richard to keep warm. As evening approached, they stopped to have a quick snack before it was time to head for the theatre. Neither of them was very hungry so a coffee and a biscotti in a café was all they needed. As they were sitting in the café, Helen excused herself. Whilst she was away, Richard was thinking about moving on to the theatre and suddenly started to panic that the bucket shop tickets might be restricted view. Everything else today had been so wonderful and he didn't want that to stop. When Helen returned Richard thought she looked radiant, she had obviously titivated her make-up in the rest room. He pulled her close as she sat down and kissed her on the cheek and as he did so he was engulfed by the newly applied perfume that so reminded him of her.

Richard's fears were unfounded and again he thought someone on high must indeed have been intervening as the theatre seats he had bought from the bucket shop were perfectly placed in the stalls. Nevertheless, he made a mental note to himself to make better plans in the future. Helen loved dancing and the show was exactly the kind of performance she liked to see, although afterwards she teased Richard about why he took her to see scantily clad young ladies. Richard blushed, but she soon put him out of his misery with a great big thank you kiss fully on the lips as they left the theatre. From there, they took a taxi back to the flat in St John's Wood where they stayed the night together.

The next day they woke quite late and were lying in bed cuddling each other but moving towards intimacy when the campanologists suddenly began. Richard started laughing.

"What's so funny?" Helen asked, laughing too at Richard's infectious mirth. When he had regained control, Richard explained about his parents' quality time on a Sunday morning, how they never went to Church, but that a family friend always took Richard. They both laughed again as Helen also recalled her own parents' methods of getting time to themselves although until that moment she had not considered it. They got up later in the morning and spent the rest of the day loafing around reading the papers before returning to Cambridge together in the evening in Helen's car.

8

For Richard the next week dragged. He was not seeing Helen as she was off with her Institute at a conference at Finlandia Hall in Helsinki until the following Sunday. Being at a loose end and eager in any case to get back to St John's Wood to be on his own again to be able to listen to the remainder of the file, Richard decided to take Friday as a research day in London. Excusing himself from work and turning down an offer from his assistant, David, to join him, he set off on Thursday evening after a fleeting visit to his parents. They were both well and preparing for a holiday. 'Again' thought Richard, although he didn't really begrudge them their indulgences. This time they were off to the Caribbean for a cruise. His visit was partly selfish in that it saved him the need to cook for himself, but also he thought by visiting them that day, they would be unlikely to disturb him the following day which would leave him free to concentrate on listening to his grandfather's file, of which his parents knew nothing.

Following the early dinner, Richard set off. He chose to travel by train and his father dropped him at the station just in time to catch a fast train to King's Cross. From there it was just a short Underground trip on the Circle Line to Baker Street and then north on the Jubilee Line to St John's Wood. His apartment was only a two-minute walk from the art deco Underground Station.

He arrived at about nine forty-five and after making himself some tea, settled down to watch the BBC's Ten O'clock News. Most of the news just washed over him as he was slightly fatigued from the trip, but there was a review of the conference that Helen had gone to which took his interest. The commentary was suggesting that hypnosis had far more to offer with regard to treatments and cures of ailments than had been appreciated to date and that there were several leading authorities on the subject from all over the world attending the convention who claimed to be close to discovering new ways of treating patients. There were also sceptics who for the most part were doctors unable or unwilling to accept that the brain could overcome problems without the intervention of medicine. Richard was most interested in this and sent a text to Helen asking her to take good notes on the debate so he could consider the arguments; after all it was a topical subject for him, but he had no idea of just how relevant it would become. As he watched the local news and weather he became aware he was drifting off to sleep, so after washing up he retired to bed where he slipped into a broken sleep interrupted by the refuge collectors' early round the next morning.

He awoke almost as tired as when he had gone to bed and after lying there for a while, listening to the background music of the radio, he rose and made himself some tea and breakfast before dressing. Almost as soon as he completed that his thoughts turned to the remainder of the file. He could wait no longer; he had to know its secrets. Moving to the living room he ordered the multi-media system to start up and move to his grandfather's file, which he then set to play from where he had left off the previous Saturday.

"Hello again Richard," said the unmistakable digital voice of his grandfather, "interesting wasn't it."

"What?" said Richard somewhat taken aback at the personal nature of what he was thinking his grandfather was referring to after listening to the first part of the file, i.e. his intimate weekend with Helen.

"The news item last night on hypnosis."

"Yes, yes it was extremely interesting and I sent a text to Hel... why am I telling you that? You already know," said Richard still not used to this future knowledge thing. "Does that have any relevance to anything you are going to tell me?"

"What makes you think I have anything to tell you?"

"Well, you always used to send me off to do my research before you initiated me into a new subject," Richard replied, pleased that he had deduced that, or at least he thought he had deduced that. He wasn't really sure anymore about whether his thoughts were his or somehow pre-planned.

"You are correct Richard, I do have something to tell you and it is this..."

Richard sat forward to listen to what his grandfather was about to say.

"Richard, earlier, I told you that I would give you the knowledge to access the ninety percent of the brain

that is currently not used by humankind and in turn the key to a far longer life."
Richard nodded in agreement and said, "Yes."
"As you know, I have asked you to research hypnosis and hypnotherapy practices. The reason for this is that hypnosis is the key to humankind accessing the part of the brain that is currently unavailable to them, the latent brain if you like. I am going to tell you how to change that to an embryonic stage that, with time and training, will provide access to most of the remainder of the brain, bringing a wealth of information, insight, processing, understanding and a highly developed intellect."
Not wanting to disturb his grandfather's monologue, Richard wrote on his pad 'access to most of the remainder' as, amongst many other things at present, he did not understand why it should not be access to all the brain's power. As he put down the pencil and sat back again, his grandfather said, "No need to write Richard, I will explain all of your questions as they arise, don't write them down and I will deal with them there and then. The reason that you will never have full access to the brain in normal use is that there needs to be a reserve for use in emergencies. A reserve, if you like, for use in times when survival may be an issue for example and you need to call on that little extra bit of brain processing power. From your research you will have learnt that there are some people in the world that already have access to a small part of the potential brain beyond the currently considered normal usage, but they are few and far between and have no real understanding of why they can do this, or how. They, and others, consider this a gift rather than a right.

These people are generally able to perform self-hypnosis although they may not be aware that is what they are doing."
Richard interrupted, "How do you perform self-hypnosis without reference to a hypnotist?" He thought he had learnt that much from Helen who had explained she listened to the recording of another hypnotherapist. Immediately, his grandfather continued by explaining that, "Everyone is capable of performing a form of self-hypnosis, albeit at a very low level. For instance, a woman in a noisy room concentrating on reading a book, but oblivious to all around her is in a low level of self-hypnosis. This state can be broken by a louder than usual noise, a move by another person into her personal space, or simply talking to her directly could also re-awaken her mind to the here and now, as all these scenarios could be a threat to her person and even in hypnosis you are alert to attack or undesired mental manipulation by others."
Carrying on, Richard's grandfather talked briefly about how hypnosis was currently being used in controlling habits such as smoking and drinking and also to overcome phobias, all of which Richard by now was quite familiar with.
"You will remember," his grandfather continued, "that under hypnosis, to alter future behaviour, you are asked to access the 'control room' of your mind and change 'switches' there. This process is extremely successful if the person under hypnosis wants to be receptive. It is however much more far-reaching than anyone realises at present."
'At last,' Richard thought, 'I am going to find out the secret from beyond the grave.' He sat up and leant

forward to listen even more intently as his grandfather carried on.

"As I have said, in a state of hypnosis a person, let's call her Paula, who is willing to change herself mentally is able to do just that by accessing her control room and changing switches. However, at the normal level of hypnosis, these switches are sliding controls with one end of the switch being 'off' and the other end 'on', similar to a sound control box in a studio. There is the possibility therefore for the level of change to be on a sliding scale between zero and 100%. Thus, a change may not only be partial, the degree being controlled by Paula, but that type of control also permits the change to be reversed without her knowledge or desire with the control slipping back to its previous level. Thus, as this is a mental process unconsciously controlled by the mind, the changes are sometimes not completely successful or permanent. The solution to this"...

'Here it comes.' thought Richard, now on the very edge of his seat.

"... is to not change the switches at the level of hypnosis where the switches are sliding controls but to access the sub-hypnosis level where the switches are either 'On' or 'Off' with no ability for them to self-reverse or to be partially on."

As Richard pushed back on his seat and opened his mouth to speak, his grandfather said, "You are now asking yourself how we access the sub-hypnosis level of consciousness." Richard nodded.

"It is relatively simple, but to date no-one has thought of it as it is beyond the level of intelligence they currently hold. What is required is a second hypnotherapist to take over from the first when Paula is under hypnosis to take her to the next level, the sub-hypnosis level of consciousness. The process is almost the same as to the hypnosis level but must be undertaken by a second hypnotherapist and of the opposite sex to Paula. I say the process is almost the same, the difference is only one of terminology. Instead of talking to the subconscious the second hypnotherapist is talking to the base-consciousness, the very root being, the DNA, where the control switches are much more basic, on or off, much like binary code, 0 or 1. That is the language they will talk in that will allow access to this level, the syntax is beyond the mind of anyone at present."

Richard could no longer keep quiet, "But how does that help, except to make the changes more permanent and irreversible? How does that affect brainpower and mortality?"

"Well my boy, we are dealing with genes and, as I said, that is either on or off. If it's defective, you want it off, if it's undesirable you want it off, but if it's off and desirable or beneficial you want it on. Under your direction, the human race will be able to control this." He paused, "Let me explain, its not as simple as you think."

Richard raised his eyebrows, he didn't think it was simple, all of this was taxing even his brilliant brain."

His grandfather continued, "It will very soon be realised that there is a sub-level to a gene, a nano-gene cluster that allows finer control of a gene. The control there is also on/off, but in the way of dip switches on a computer, a group of three within one gene, allowing a further level of control. Using binary, that gives seven levels of control for each gene. The changes therefore offer a sliding scale of effectiveness to the gene but with certainty that it will not self-alter later."

Richard was struggling to keep up, this was not his field of expertise, although he understood the analogy, which helped.

"It is the key to controlling DNA, thus the key to a disease free life. However, before you can do this or even tell the world about it, you must first improve the intellect of the human race, as otherwise these techniques could be used for devious purposes. It will take many years of brain training before everyone is up to speed and only then can you release the news of sub-hypnosis' full power. This will allow the human brain to come to terms with the new level of IQ before they have to deal with longer life too. So, I am going to show you how to access the remainder of the brain's processing power, or at least 90% of it, a reverse of the position the human race has now, in fact. Before anyone can begin brain training, under sub-hypnosis they will need to make changes to the switches that control all the sectors of the brain to enable them. Before you ask, as no one is at present capable of speaking binary, Helen will have to be the first to be base-altered. I will act as the second to get into her base consciousness and allow her to make the necessary changes to her brain sector switches."

"H-h-helen?" Richard spluttered surprised, sitting bolt upright and suddenly, and temporarily, returning to his stutter.

"You see Richard," his grandfather chuckled, "these sliding switches sometimes allow a backslide. Yes Helen, who else? It has to be her first, then you."

"Me?" asked Richard, "I'm not sure about this. In any case, how will you sub-hypnotise Helen, no-one else knows at present, who will take her to the first level, if you do the second part?"
His grandfather continued, undaunted by Richard's perceptible shock, "No, she is very good at self-hypnosis and can bring herself to a deep enough first-level of hypnosis and then I can take over. The only criterion is that the second level of hypnosis must be carried out by someone of the opposite sex so she can self-hypnotise to the first level. When both of you are base altered, you can begin training your brains to their ultimate level. You are both very smart already, it won't take long, perhaps a month."
Richard, not for the first time recently, was almost speechless, all he could utter was, "A month, a month!"
"Yes," said his grandfather, "about a month for your current level of IQ. Training times will vary and so will final IQ levels. There will still be hierarchy although not with such a wide percentage gap between the top and the bottom, so communication will be much more rational; that is very important. Equally important to remember in all of this, however, is that whilst you can change your switches and your DNA, you cannot change fate. Although peoples' lives will be very significantly increased in length, accidents will still happen that will bring some lives to a premature end. There could also still be famine and diseases that may kill before a solution is found, despite the increased intellect."
"Okay Grandad, but how do I go about all of this? I'm not sure I can convince Helen on this."
His grandfather responded and Richard could almost sense a smile on the old man's face, "You will my dear

boy, you will convince her, trust me. As for how to go forward, I want you to set up an institute worldwide - 'The Stuart Harper Institute for Neural Engineering' or SHINE for short. In my will, I have left you a substantial amount of money to start this off. I suggest that the institute should be in London with clinics to follow in major towns all over the world. 'And where is the money going to come from for that?' you are now thinking. Well, once you have set up the first few clinics, governments all over the world will become interested and they will fund future clinics. However, you must maintain control or there could be skulduggery. To assist you to do that, you must have the majority shareholding in each clinic. I therefore have a schedule of stocks and shares for you and their future values to allow you to invest with a guaranteed return. You simply need to invest enough money at the right time to keep ahead of the monetary requirement for each clinic."

"Is that not illegal?" asked Richard.

"No-one except you will know, and in any event it is necessary for the future of the World. In fact if you look at the statutes you may find there isn't one that forbids getting information from the future. Anyway, call it retribution against the bankers for when they were ripping everyone off in 2009. You are simply recovering what rightfully belonged to the investors who lost money and taxpayers who had to dig more deeply into their pockets and putting that money to very good use. Don't give it another thought," said his grandfather. "You just need to account for every penny and it will be okay, trust me, I know."

Richard's head by now was spinning. He had not even dreamt that he would be so involved and inextricably linked to what he thought could only be described as the future of mankind.

"I must leave now, Grandad; I have to think about all of this and also decide how to break the news to Helen. Oh, Helen, how will I do that, how will I tell her, does she have to be first?"

"Yes, she does. You cannot be base altered until she learns DNA binary and as I told you, she will be fine about it, don't forget that hypnosis is her work, it will excite her to be a part of this, and it will be a challenge for her, she loves a challenge. I will speak to you again when you are ready, goodbye my boy."

The room fell silent save for the faint hum of Richard's multimedia system. Richard's brain was pounding and at that very moment he wished he already had the extra brainpower to absorb all that he had been told by his grandfather that morning. So tired was he that he fell into a long deep sleep as he contemplated what he had been told, only waking at 6:00 p.m., when the phone rang. It was Helen reminding him that they were going to her parents' house the next day for lunch. They also discussed the details of her return from Helsinki early in the next morning when Richard was going to collect her from the airport. Richard was quiet on the phone and Helen by now knew him well enough to know something was up, however she decided it best not to talk about it on the phone, but to wait until they met. She was however, concerned that something was bothering him, as he was usually so upbeat about life.

She had a sleepless night that night thinking about what it might be.

9

As usual on Sundays Richard was awakened by the church bell ringers; but as he had taken a long time to get to sleep and had then slept poorly, he was not as cheered as he normally was by their sound. Having slept most of the previous afternoon probably didn't help, he thought, but also his mind was running through the scenarios his grandfather had set out for him the day before. He was also thinking through what he was going to say to Helen, as he was about to go and collect her. He was wondering how he would break the news to her. He knew she would know something was up with him. She always did these days. He lay in bed for a short while just listening to the bells, eventually laughing to himself that one of the operators was definitely not pulling from the same hymn sheet, as his or her bell was always late. It was supposed to be the last bell in the sequence, but was so late it sounded like it was the first in the next.

After a few more minutes Richard rose and went through his usual ablutions, taking a little more care than usual to coordinate his clothes as he prepared to travel to Heathrow T5 to collect Helen. As he was shaving, he thought, 'Terminal 5, what a nightmare, I think I'll go by train, it'll be easier than driving'. He also didn't want to put his car into a multi-storey car park where it could get damaged. He had a 1999 Aston Martin DB7 Vantage Volante in British Racing Green that was in pristine conditio,n that he kept at St John's Wood in the secure parking he had there. He had always been a bit of a petrol-head and this car was his pride and joy and wherever he went he always had a problem finding somewhere to park it safely, free from potential damage. 'I could come back for that after meeting Helen', he thought. Grabbing his British Racing Green Aston Martin umbrella from the stand in the hallway he set off.

The walk from his apartment to the station was only a minute or so and within another two he was on the Jubilee Line travelling south to Oxford Circus where he could pick up the Piccadilly Line to T5. It wasn't a long journey and he was soon settled in a seat on the Pic' Line when suddenly he remembered what his grandfather had said. He was so immersed in his thoughts on this that when the T5 station came up he almost missed the stop. Dashing off the train just as the doors closed, he realised he had left his umbrella on the train, but luck must have been with him that day as the train's doors re-opened due to someone having trapped their suitcase in the doors further down the carriage. Richard jumped back on the train, retrieved his umbrella and jumped off again as the doors slammed behind him. He was now a little flustered, but very pleased not to have lost his favourite umbrella.

'Onward', he thought as he ascended into the T5 concourse to find the Arrivals area. His timing had been good, the flight had landed from Helsinki only ten minutes before and its baggage was in the hall. He bought himself a strong cappuccino to go and leant against a column outside the arrivals door waiting for Helen, again drifting into thought about his grandfather's file.

As the doors from the arrivals hall opened for what seemed to Richard to be the 100th time, Helen was there beaming at him, but with her head tilted to the side slightly, a sure sign to him that she knew something was amiss. His face lit up as he saw her and the two of them embraced and kissed warmly for a few seconds before they looked at each other closely. At that moment Richard realised, and could not believe, how much he had missed her but it was Helen who voiced this sentiment to him and all he could then say was "me too." He thought that this was not the welcome he would have chosen to have given her and said, "I really missed you," hugging her again and lifting her off the floor. An elderly lady who was passing by chuckled to herself and said "I wish my husband would do that to me". At this they both laughed although Richard was a little embarrassed, as evidenced by his blushing cheeks. Picking up her case, Richard said, "Let's go, we have to get back to St John's Wood to pick up my car then to your parents' place." As they walked off he told her about nearly losing his umbrella.

The trip back to his flat seemed to be over in a trice as they were so busy catching up with each other's news during their short time apart. This time, as they got off the train, Richard remembered his umbrella and it was a good job he did, as outside the station the rain was tipping down. They walked back to the flat with Richard carrying the small case and Helen holding the umbrella between them. It seemed to offer little protection, but they didn't really care, they were again together. As they arrived at the flat, Helen decided she would like to freshen up before they left for her parents' house in Cambridge and was about to move to the bedroom, but not before she had sent a parting question to Richard, one he had been dreading.

"So, what's up, you seem slightly preoccupied?"

'Slightly,' he thought, 'more than slightly!' But he said only "It's nothing, really," sounding less than convincing.

"I know you," she said, "I know that look. Do you want to tell me; is it to do with your grandfather?"

He looked up in amazement, with his mouth open, how did she know?

"It is, isn't it?"

Richard looked down and nodded at the same time.

"Do you want to talk about it?"

Richard realised that Helen thought he was sad about his grandfather's death. 'Of course, how could she know about the files', he thought.

"No, it's okay, I'm fine. You go and get yourself ready, we can talk later," Richard said, turning on the multimedia system and ordering it to TV as if to stop the conversation. Fifteen minutes later Helen returned to the lounge where Richard was watching a current affairs programme. Or at least that's what he appeared to be doing to Helen, but when she asked him what it was about, Richard had no idea, again fuelling Helen's belief that he was indeed preoccupied. However, she said nothing, no doubt he would tell her when he was ready.

They left the flat and went down to the car park where the Aston was parked. Helen had not seen the Aston before. Its interior was two-tone green and tan leather complementing the British Racing green paintwork and a green mohair convertible soft-top hood, a mixture that didn't impress Helen at all, but she had the tact not to say too much as she knew it would upset Richard. He had previously talked to her about the car with such passion. Looking at the colour combination reminded her of how he put his wardrobe together which made her smile broadly. Richard took that as appreciation of the car and she was happy for him to think that. Richard opened the passenger door for Helen, who eased herself into the figure-hugging bucket seat being careful that her handbag did not catch on any of the rich walnut trim. He then walked round to the driver's side, climbed into his cockpit, sat for a moment or two then he hit the large red starter button, firing the engine into life. Being in the garage the noise was very loud which brought a smile to Richard's face temporarily allowing him to forget his dilemma of how to tell Helen of her part in his grandfather's plan. She was less impressed by the sound of the engine, but again said nothing. As they pulled out of the garage the noise was less strident, which pleased her no end. By now the rain had subsided and Richard said, "Not such a bad day on balance, shall I put the roof down?"
She just looked at him as if to say, 'are you mad?' He had been joking, it was only about 8 degrees and he had

set himself a rule of not putting the roof down below 11. He sped off up the road laughing as he went.

The trip to Cambridge took just over an hour as traffic on the M11 was light and the rain held off for the entire journey. As he drove, Richard was thinking that he would have to wash the car as soon as he arrived because the spray from the road was making his pride and joy dirty. Helen was thinking, perhaps the car is not so bad in spite of everything, it certainly was comfortable, even at speed and, with the hood up, surprisingly quiet. They didn't talk much as Richard was thinking about how he was going to break his news to Helen and she drifted into sleep in the warm comfort of the heated seat as Richard drove. She had not slept well whilst away.

Arriving at Cambridge, Richard dropped Helen off at her parent's house first before he drove to his parents' house to park his car in the safety of their garage. Richard's parents were away until later in the week, but they had a large, underused garage in any case, so he always had somewhere safe to park. On the way he took the car to a hand car wash round the corner from his parents' house. It pleased him to see it pristine again. After parking the car and locking up, he walked to Helen's parents' house picking up some flowers on the way. This time they were indeed for Janet as she was cooking dinner for him and Helen. As he stood there at the door of their house wiping his left shoe on the back of his right trouser leg the door opened. It was Jim, who Richard remembered from seeing him through

the half open door when he had picked Helen up before.
"Hello young man," he said stepping out to greet Richard with a firm handshake. Richard swapped the flowers to his left hand, shook his hand and responded, "Hello Sir."
"Oh no need for the Sir, Jim will do," Jim laughed as he spoke "we're pretty informal here. Come in my boy, come in, it's good to meet you at last."
As Richard walked through the door, Helen was coming down the stairs looking radiant in another change of clothes, "I see you've met Dad then," she said smiling at Richard. "You didn't need to bring him flowers."
"No, no they're for your Mum," Richard said, immediately feeling foolish, realising she was teasing him. Janet was in the kitchen preparing dinner and she shouted through to Helen to take Richard through to the lounge, which she did. As they sat, Janet came into the lounge too and thanked Richard for the flowers when he handed them to her. As they all sat in the lounge, Richard was feeling awkward and Helen realised this and tried to put him at ease by asking him if he would like a drink. Jim jumped up and said, "I will do it darling". He suggested wine and everyone agreed, so he set off to find some. Helen could see that her mother was bursting to ask Richard some questions and tried to parry this by saying to Richard, "Have you noticed the rosettes? Mum trains horses and shows them, she's won all of these over the years."
"Yes, I did notice them," Richard said, not really telling the truth, "Do you still train them?" he continued trying to sound interested.

"Oh no, not so much now," said Janet. It's very hard work and I'm not so young any more."
"You're not old," said Richard, suddenly realising he was possibly playing with fire, but he got away with it as Janet smiled and said, "I like him Helen, he can stay."
"Mum!" Helen exclaimed, embarrassed by her. Jim returned with the drinks, which helped the moment to move on.
"I'll just go and see how dinner is doing," said Janet, "it should be ready in about ten minutes or so."
"Great." said Jim "I'm ready for it, are you Richard?"
"Yes." Richard replied, "I haven't eaten today since breakfast."
"You should take more care of yourself Richard," said Janet.
"Mum!" Helen exclaimed, again.
Janet left the room.

"I hear you have a fantastic car, Richard," said Jim breaking the silence that had fallen on the room save for the background noise of Janet clinking plates and cutlery in the dining room.
"An Aston Martin isn't it?"
"Yes," replied Richard enthused that Jim had an interest in cars, "It's a 1999 DB7 convertible, and it's only done 6,000 miles."
Helen thought how nice it was that Richard and her dad were talking about a common interest, even if she did not exactly share it. At least it was a safe subject that should not embarrass her. They continued to talk cars until Janet came in to announce dinner in the dining room.

"Oooh, the dining room, there's posh, we normally use the breakfast room," said Jim. After he said it he realised he really should have known better as Janet gave him a look that could have killed a velociraptor. He was more careful after that knowing that would not be the last of it. They all sat down and Janet served up the first course, Stilton and broccoli soup, one of her specialities.
When all were served Janet sat down and said, "Well, Richard, it's nice to meet you properly at last, you are very welcome here."
"Thank you, Janet, it's good to meet you too," Richard replied, adding that the soup was delicious. Helen had felt that she had been very quiet since Richard arrived; on edge, waiting for her mother to start the questioning and she did not have to wait long as Janet said, "So, Richard," a clear sign to Helen and Jim that the inquisition was about to commence, "I believe you are in research?" She had been harbouring that question since it went unanswered when they first met over two months previously and were interrupted by Helen at the time before she could get a response.
"Yes," Richard replied as he explained how he had been researching with his grandfather who was of course known by reputation to Helen's parents. Both of Helen's parents expressed sorrow to Richard and Helen feared that this would bring him down again to where he was earlier that day, but it did not and she was thankful for that.

The rest of dinner was served with a roast main course and home-made ice-cream to finish and during the meal Janet's questions continued thick and fast. Richard answered them all, parrying some he cared not to answer. Helen was as embarrassed as she had expected to be, but at least it was now over; the first meeting between any boyfriend and her mother was a nightmare for her, not that she had had many. Helen's father was allowed to ask the occasional question too, but his didn't embarrass Helen. Through Jim's questions, one thing they did find out was that Jim and Richard's father James, apart from having the same first name had been at senior school together. It didn't click initially when Jim heard the name James Harper because at school James was known by his middle name Alex, as there were three James' in the class. Richard couldn't wait to see his dad's reaction when he mentioned that Jim Harrison was Helen's father. Richard also found out that Jim was an architect with his own business in Cambridge. Richard found architecture interesting and Jim promised to take him on an architectural trip round Cambridge sometime, something he would look forward to. Helen was really pleased that her dad and Richard had got on so well. Richard thanked Janet and Jim for their hospitality and he left to retire to his flat to prepare and be ready for the day ahead at what was now his research facility.

Helen saw Richard to the door, kissed him warmly as he left and thanked him for being so understanding and answering all her mother's prying questions. "She's fine, Helen, not nearly as bad as you made out."
"That's easy for you to say," said Helen. "Bye Richard," she continued.
"Bye Helen," he replied as he left the house and walked home.

Within seconds of leaving he was in deep thought again as to how to break the news to Helen about her part in the grand plan. His trip home took no time at all and upon arrival he prepared his notes for his current research project before retiring to bed for what was to be another restless night. Richard was beginning to have serious doubts about the ethics of what he was being asked to do and before he conveyed the information to Helen, he needed to speak with his grandfather's file again.

10

It was about 6:00 a.m. when Richard decided to stop trying to sleep any more. He had had a terrible night and could no longer put off getting answers to his numerous questions. He dragged himself from his bed, the covers of which were all knotted up as a result of his tossing and turning all night. In the kitchen he prepared a cup of tea and in his dressing gown went to the lounge where he commanded his multimedia system to start up.

"System on," he said. "Play grandfather's file from where it last stopped."

Immediately the file opened and said "Hello Richard, I've been expecting you."

"Hello Grandad, I have some deep concerns, but you already know that don't you?"

"Yes I do," the voice continued.

"You are worried that this is reminiscent of something akin to Hitler's dream of changing people into his view of the perfect race? However, it is not like that at all. You are forgetting that in this instance it needs the approval of the people before they can be changed and it applies to all, not just a select few."

"Yes," replied Richard, "but what about the ones who cannot be hypnotised, the twenty percent or so; they will not benefit and will be left behind both in terms of intelligence and lifespan. How will they cope? And their families, they will lose them at what will become an early age."
"No," his grandfather interjected, "not an early age, the normal age when they would otherwise have died and they will not be epsilons, merely left with their born intelligence, although admittedly not as intelligent as their peers will become. The other thing to consider is that people will have choices. The partner of someone who cannot be hypnotised has the option not to take part in the neural engineering thus keeping in line with them."
"But what about the future, surely beings who cannot be hypnotised will continue to be born?" said Richard still concerned.
"No my boy, hypnosis of the parents after conception will allow neural engineering of the children before they are born and still in their mother's womb, so the mother will control the hypnosis and change the DNA of the unborn child sufficiently, and only, to allow hypnosis of the child in the future, thus it will maintain its right to choose to take part or not."
"But what about the children of the ones who cannot take part. They have a one in five chance of not being able to be hypnotised."
His grandfather took over the conversation, "And in the next generation a one in 25 chance and beyond that 1 in 125 and so on reducing all the time. Look upon it as a current disease that is slowly being eradicated. In five generations time the chances of a child being born that

is incapable of being hypnotised will be less than 0.03%. That's less than, or similar to, the risk of some current abnormalities we accept every day in childbirth. So you see, you are not thinking rationally. Take some more time if you need it, but think it through. It will be for the benefit of mankind at the end of the day, Richard and that has always come with some risk. That is not to say that this won't be undertaken carefully. When hypnotherapists are brain-trained they will be able to learn to speak in DNA binary; you do not want just anyone being able to do this. There is of course a safeguard in that a person cannot be forced to do anything they do not want to do under hypnosis; however, at the next level, under sub-hypnosis, that is not true. The hypnotherapist has complete and utter control so a very careful vetting process must take place to ensure there is no subversive action."

Richard, with the feeling he had somehow just been told off, said, "Sorry, Grandad, you're right, I am not thinking this through am I?"

"Also, my boy, I have seen the future and it is good. This works well for you all. I only wish I could have been part of it in my lifetime."

At that Richard was suddenly reminded that his grandfather was dead. At the same time, he also thought that to date only he had heard the file and he started worrying that this was not in fact happening and that it was all in his head. The dog nearly being run over could have been in his head, but how then would he have known he was going to meet Helen? Could he have created that himself too? More confusion. The proof for him then would be if Helen believed him. He decided he had to progress this and soon, for the sake of his sanity.

By now it was 6:45 a.m. and Richard said goodbye again to his grandfather, thanking him for the chat. His grandfather told him that he was there for him anytime. As Richard changed the system to TV to catch the breakfast news he was still thinking about the best way to tell Helen. As he pondered, a news item on the TV extolled the virtue of a mini break in London. Richard, although deep in thought, caught the concept and thought 'that's it, we can go to the London flat this weekend and I can tell Helen then'. He would have the file there too so he could get her to listen to it to prove he wasn't going mad. It would also be a good opportunity to return the Aston to London.

Richard, now re-enthused, proceeded to get ready for work and was at his laboratory by about 8:00 a.m. somewhat earlier than usual. This did not go unnoticed by many of the early birds who passed the usual comments like, 'Hi Richard, you're early, did you fall out of bed?' and 'Did you sleep here this weekend?' He was not amused however as he had a lot to do if he was to have Friday afternoon off. He knew that Helen would be free then, as she always tried to work only four days, Monday to Thursday, but he called her just to confirm. She was okay for that and very much looking forward to going to London again. Richard told her he had something to discuss with her and that he proposed to do that on Saturday at the flat in St. John's Wood. She was impatient to know what it was but he simply said he would have to prepare for the discussion so didn't want to pre-empt it.

"It's in relation to hypnosis, a theory I've been researching," he said.
She was temporarily appeased by that, but was very curious as to what it was that Richard had been working on.

The week passed slowly and Richard had his head down into work so didn't see Helen until Friday. This was somewhat unusual, but Helen put it down to Richard's research. The truth of the matter was that Richard was not looking forward to explaining what he needed to explain and therefore decided that absence was the best policy. On Friday afternoon Richard left his flat in Cambridge, picked up his car from his parents' house (they were still away) and drove to Helen's to pick her up. She was ready and waiting for him. Her parents were out, so she checked the house, locked up and got into the Aston. Without much of a greeting Richard set off down the road in the direction of London. After a period of silence Helen looked at him and said:
"Have I done something wrong?"
"No, of course not."
"Then why are you not talking to me, you didn't even greet me properly earlier."
"I know, I'm sorry Helen, it's this research I've been doing. It's quite intense and all consuming. I'm sorry, I'll try to forget it for a while."
Richard spotted a lay-by and decided to stop. He pulled up and turned the engine off, leant over to her and gave her the hug he felt he should have given her earlier, to which she responded nearly immediately.
"That's better," she said. "But what is it that's getting you in such a state, I've not seen you like this before."

"It's the work my grandfather was researching. It's taking me to the edge of my knowledge and understanding, really complicated stuff with many moral issues to add to the dilemma. I'll explain more tomorrow, but in the meantime I'll try to forget it, I'm sorry."
Helen was relieved that it was only work, but was nevertheless concerned that he had got himself into such a state about it. They continued the drive listening to music they both liked in not quite silence; a quiet mood, but both were happy with that now.

The roads were quite busy as they approached London, but the journey was still quite a quick one. At the flat Richard parked the car in his normal spot in the garage and they ascended the lift to the penthouse. Once there, Richard turned the heating up and lit the gas coal-effect fire in the lounge, as it was early Spring and the temperature outside was only in the low teens. The rooms however, warmed quickly.
"This used to be a real coal fire, it was wonderful," said Richard, "but my Mum had it converted as it was not really practical in a penthouse."
"I bet it was because she was the one who had to clean the ash out and set it," replied Helen smiling.
"You're right, it was. No servants now you see," Richard joked.
"Yes," said Helen, "these flats are beautiful and must have been really splendid in the days when there were servants when they were built. What are they, 1910?"
"Yes, spot on said Richard, your Dad has taught you well".

Helen laughed, "It's on the building as you come in, and there is a plaque showing the date the foundation stone was laid. Have you never noticed?"
"No," Richard replied, "none out of ten for observation then?"
"Exactly," Helen said as she moved towards him for a hug. Richard obliged.

They went out to eat in the West End that night to another splendid building, the Wolseley Restaurant in Piccadilly.
"It used to be a car showroom," said Richard ardently.
"Trust you to know that said Helen, but when was it built?"
They both laughed. Celebrities often used the restaurant, but if there were any in that night neither noticed as they only had eyes for each other. They left the restaurant at a little after 10:00 p.m. and headed the short distance home by cab to the flat. The flat was warm and welcoming and Richard had managed to keep his mind on Helen and not the matter he would be telling her about the next day. They had had a good night and they retired to bed together and after making love tenderly, soon sank into a deep sleep in each other's arms.

11

In the morning there were no church bells, it being a Saturday, but they were awakened at about nine in any event by a call from Richard's mother announcing that she and his father were back from the latest trip. 'Thank goodness Helen didn't answer' he thought as he spoke to his mother asking how their trip went and how his dad was. All was fine and they ended their conversation agreeing he would see them the following weekend at their house on Easter Sunday for lunch and he was to bring Helen too.

Awake by now, they got up, showered, dressed, had some breakfast and settled down in the lounge in front of the fire.
"So, Richard, what's this all about then, it sounds most intriguing," Helen asked, clasping both of her arms around one of his. So here it was, the moment Richard had been dreading for a while now, upon him. How to start? Even though he had run it through his mind on numerous occasions before now, the time was here. 'How to start? Well, here goes' he thought.
"Helen," he hesitated as he spoke, "in my life, this is one of the most difficult things I have ever had to

explain to anyone. The ramifications of this research, if implemented, are absolutely immense for the whole of mankind." He continued without waiting for any comment from Helen. "You knew my grandfather and his interest in your field of work." "Yes." she replied.

"Well, he was working on something very big, very big indeed in terms of life as we know it. I have discovered some unfinished research of his on a computer file whereby he believes that it is possible to increase our IQ's and extend human life using new and currently unexploited hypnosis and hypnotherapy techniques. He uses the term 'base consciousness', does that mean anything to you?"

Helen was now looking very serious and replied, "Yes, he had mentioned this as a concept to me when I met him to discuss hypnosis. Like you, he wanted knowledge about it."

"Good," said Richard, "that's a start at least. What about 'base-altered' and 'DNA binary' do they mean anything to you?"

"No, nothing," she responded, shrugging her shoulders.

"Okay," said Richard as he realised now what he needed to explain.

Over the next two hours or so Richard brought Helen up to speed on the research that his grandfather had divulged to him, but for the time being, as he had been asked to do by his grandfather, he didn't mention the file with his grandfather's interaction. He merely referred to the file as being his grandfather's research. He mentioned the need for different sexes of hypnotherapist at the second stage and the concept of base-altering DNA by the use of a new language of DNA binary. He didn't yet mention how this process was to start with his grandfather's tape being involved and Helen was so stunned by the whole idea that at the moment she didn't even think to ask. One thing that Helen noted, and Richard's grandfather had not mentioned it to him, he had not thought to ask was why the second level of hypnosis should need someone of the opposite sex. She guessed it was to do with X and Y chromosomes, perhaps the inability of the DNA to take instructions from the same sex as itself. She asked Richard, but he didn't know, 'A question for my grandfather next time,' he thought. Her supposition didn't make a lot of sense to Richard, but she seemed to understand it, which Richard thought was good as it showed she was already engaging with the subject. Her other questions were the very questions Richard had asked relating to the moral aspects and Richard was able to answer these as he had discussed the issues with his grandfathers file, but of course he could not provide Helen with that proof at this stage. He at least had been able to speak with the file for reassurance and he was aware he was having trouble here. He had only known Helen for three months, but could sense her unease. They decided to stop talking about this for a while and return to it after Helen had had time to reflect over lunch, which they had delivered in, as there was no food in the flat. Richard made them both a cappuccino whilst they waited for the food to arrive from a little Italian restaurant at Swiss Cottage, not far from the flat.

The food arrived at about 1:00 p.m. and they both tried to eat, but had so much on their minds they drifted back into discussing the DNA alteration in the base consciousness, that Richard decided to call ‘SHINE Therapy’ after he explained to Helen his grandfather’s wish that he set up the SHINE Clinics. Helen was sceptical as to where the money would come from for all of this even after hearing that Sir Stuart had left a substantial amount of money in his will to allow it to happen. She knew from the ‘Sunday Times Rich List’ roughly how much Sir Stuart had and despite it being many millions of pounds, she didn’t think it would go far on something like this. However, of greater concern to her were the moral issues. She voiced the same main issues as Richard had, but then suddenly she realised that, in the early days, families could be completely split by this. Mothers who could not be hypnotised producing sons and daughters who might also not be able to be hypnotised with fathers who could, resulting in members of families ageing at different rates. Also, the natural death of children, already born who could not be hypnotised, long before parents who would have to live with that for hundreds of years. To bring this to the world, and she was now realising that Richard wanted her to be in the forefront, would be a fantastic opportunity, but not without inducing human suffering. On the other hand, in the longer term, she could see that there were vast opportunities with the increased IQ and longer life and cures for diseases that currently caused pain, suffering and death. With greater understanding, perhaps, she thought, there would be fewer wars and famines, but at what price initially? All of a sudden she realised that she had drifted off into thought and that Richard had stopped talking a while ago.

“Are you okay?” he said when she looked up.

"Yes, yes I am, somewhat stunned I would say, but okay," she replied.
"So what do you think?" he asked.
"It sounds fantastic," said Helen "but not without pain."
"What is, when you are talking about such a major change to the human race?" he replied. "It will be cheaper in human terms than war and may alter the way we deal with conflict so that there are no more wars."
"Yes," said Helen "but what about the population explosion; not only will you have fewer people dying from war, there will be vastly more born if we can live ten times longer than we can at present."
"I don't think so," said Richard, "we can limit the number of babies that can be born. Originally, the reason for having large families was as a result of child mortality."
Helen interjected: "That's not the only reason people have large families and you will still have mortality as an issue; you cannot change that, people will still die in accidents."
"True, but I was going on to say that if people have much more time they may choose to have children later in life."
"Or once a century for four or five centuries," she retorted giving an alternative possibility, that Richard had not considered.
"Goodness, you're right, that is a possibility. I think we will have to limit the number of children to two," he said. "That way we will still have a population increase but it can be controlled over several hundred years."
"There will still be more people than space," replied Helen, clearly way ahead of him in the reality stakes.

She continued: "That concerns me greatly; perhaps we should only increase the IQ's and not the lifespan."
"Hmm," Richard pondered on this for a moment or two then said "No, wouldn't work. It would not take long for mankind to work out the long life part for themselves with the greater IQ. I believe it's all or nothing. So, are you in?"
"I'm not sure, it's a great responsibility," she replied looking quite worried. "I need some reassurance that I would not be creating a monster. We've criticised Hitler's appalling approach, but already we are suggesting control of the population by limiting birth to two per family."
"It worked for China a few years ago when they did it," Richard replied.
"Did it? They ended up with an ageing population with few youngsters to support them so that it became a drain on the State. I'm far from convinced, Richard. This requires far more thought and perhaps some advice from others."
"No," Richard shrieked. "No, you can't discuss this with anyone else yet. It has to stay between the three of us."
"Three of us?" She looked at him curiously. "Who else knows?"
"You, me and er, grandfather," Richard replied, realising he had let something slip that he shouldn't have.
"But Richard, your grandfather is dead so it's only two of us, right?"
"Er, yes." he responded unconvincingly.
"What is it, what's going on, I know you're covering something up, I can tell now. What is it?" demanded Helen.

Richard realised that he could not and indeed should not lie to Helen. In any event, she needed to be convinced, so he decided that he should tell her everything. He was however concerned that his grandfather had said he should not tell her initially, but then he must have known that Richard would. Then he wondered if the file would work with two of them there. If it didn't he was going to look very stupid indeed in front of the woman he loved.

"Richard, tell me what it is," Helen repeated more demandingly.

"Okay," said Richard, "I will tell you, but it is almost beyond belief; be prepared to be shocked."

Helen was mystified. "Go on," she said, now almost afraid of what she had stumbled upon.

Richard started to explain, "When my grandfather died in January, no-one was with him and his passing was unnoticed by anyone for about two hours, yet his computer continued to be under his control during this time generating in two hours about 11 hours of file time."

"How could that be?" Helen intervened. "Surely the computer's clock was wrong?"

"That's what I thought initially," said Richard, "but I checked that and it was precisely correct with half an hour of time before his death and the remaining ten and a half hours after. There was a time lapse between his death and when he stopped controlling the computer, but let me continue because I now know that this is correct. I have listened to part of the file and have conversed with it."

"Conversed?" exclaimed Helen. "How; don't you mean listened?"

"No, I mean conversed," continued Richard who by now was feeling quite uneasy talking of this. Nevertheless he continued.

"I started the file and at first there was just white noise and I was about to fast forward when suddenly the voice said 'Richard'. In disbelief, I told the computer to rewind thirty seconds. Again I heard it just when I expected to and I will never forget the words it said. They were,

'Richard .... yes it is me and I am fine. Very dead in your understanding of the word but fine, please don't worry about me. You see I am in the next stage of being, beyond life as we knew it, it does exist, the after-life'."

Helen interrupted in a cynical tone of voice, "But that's not conversing, that is listening."

Richard persisted and then explained about the little dog nearly being run over and how the file predicted that. He then relayed some of the replies he was given by the file in response to his questions. He also told Helen about the 'after-life as it was explained to him by his grandfather's file. That his grandfather was now finally at peace in a wonderful place. That he was now free of the motionless, twisted body he had had in his past life. He carried on to tell her that it was not only humans that were with his grandfather; there were animals and plants there too. Similarly to Richard when he had heard this information, Helen could not take all of it on board. She blurted out, "Stop, Richard stop, this is unbelievable."

"I told you it was," he replied, pausing his monologue as she had asked him to.

"Helen," he continued after a few moments, "all you need to know is that my grandfather has told me all of this from beyond the grave; he has given me an insight that his 'world' is similar to every being, plant or creature that ever lived being a small part, a neutron, in a larger entity, but still being a whole in itself."
He further explained that his grandfather had told him there was no religion there, no race, no disease or disfigurement, no aggression, no crime and no death and that the 'world' was ever expanding with no boundaries with freedom to pass back and forth in time without barriers.
"I know this will sound far-fetched and I don't think you will fully believe it until you have listened to the file. Perhaps now is as good a time as any to do just that," Richard said, looking at Helen who appeared rather distraught. He moved over to her and gave her a hug in an effort to try to make her feel less uneasy. In truth, that helped Richard too as he was also feeling rather delicate. But it was out now; there was no going back.
"Are you ready for the file?" he asked Helen.
She drew breath and sighed deeply. "Yes, I think so."
"Would you like a drink before we start?" he asked suddenly realising that he certainly would.
"Yes please, I'll have a glass of wine, I need it," she replied.
Richard walked to the fridge and retrieved a chilled bottle of Gavi de Gavi and two glasses. Placing them on the coffee table he poured and at the same time he spoke to his multimedia system.
"System on. Prepare to play grandfather's file from where it last stopped." Immediately the system started

up and hummed quietly in the corner awaiting further instructions.
"Why not let me hear the whole file to date?" Helen enquired.
"It won't mean anything to you Helen," Richard replied. "My grandfather has already made that quite clear to me. He will know you are here with me, he has seen our future backwards, and that is how he can know what we will say and he will respond accordingly." As he spoke, he was thinking how ridiculous that sounded, but then as if to pacify himself he thought, 'so was splitting the atom less than a hundred years ago or moon travel less than fifty years ago.' All Helen could muster, quite dumbfounded by now was, "Oh, okay then."

Together, they took a sip from their glasses and then Richard commanded the system to play whereupon it immediately said, "Hello Richard." Richard replied, "Hello Grandad, I'm sorry, I couldn't bring myself to be economic with the truth with Helen, I know you didn't want me to..." The voice on the system cut across him and said, "It's okay my boy, I know she is here too, hello Helen."
As it spoke Helen shrank back realising that what it said was in direct response to what Richard had said and it, apparently, also knew she was there.
"Helen, please don't be afraid," the voice continued. "I know that this is the right thing to do, but you are both in this together and you must have the utmost trust in each other. I don't mind really, in fact I am pleased you have told Helen. Helen, is there anything you would like to ask me so you can have absolute belief in all of this?"

Helen thought for a moment then she jumped up and walked to the window. As she looked out, she said: "A van is coming along the road outside, what you can tell me about it?"

Richard looked at her anxiously awaiting a response from his grandfather that might convince her once and for all that he was indeed conversing with a file created after he had died.

"Yes Helen," Stuart spoke to her softly, "it's a delivery van, travelling north and it has Harrods green livery; its registration plate is H412ODS." She could only just read the plate from the penthouse but that mattered not; it was indeed as the file described and exactly on cue.

"Correct!" she exclaimed in a rather surprised voice. Nevertheless, she was now almost convinced and in fact somewhat relieved that Richard was not a raving lunatic as she had been beginning to suspect, with such a fantastic and improbable story. Helen asked a few more questions and the answers to these removed her immediate doubts and worries, one of which was whether she should hear the first part of the file. Stuart told her that as Richard had said, it would not now be interactive, nevertheless he agreed that it would be useful for her to hear some of the answers to the questions Richard had asked as he learnt about neural engineering. Stuart reiterated the need for secrecy about the entire matter and stressed that for the present time no-one except the three of them must know. Helen smiled at Richard when Stuart said this, as they were the very words he had used earlier that led to her being told more: 'it has to stay between the three of us'. Helen and Richard took their leave from the file and Richard shut down the multimedia system. Both of them were so absolutely and completely drained they just sat there very close to each other for a while in silence. It was Helen who spoke first saying, "I now understand why you have been so distant over the past few weeks. Please Richard, if you ever have any worries ever again, tell me, don't let me be wondering what is going on in your mind in the way I have been. It's much healthier for both of us to discuss such worries."

Richard agreed that he would and said, "I wanted to tell you, but I thought you would think me barking mad which was a possibility that had occurred to me. I thought, what if the file had not worked when you were here?"

Helen covered his lips with her hand to stop him talking and said, "Well, it has and I now know about it and believe it, so you're not mad, well not too mad," she teased, poking him in the ribs. He flinched and hugged her so she would stop. They laughed then kissed.

After a while they decided to leave the flat to take their minds off their all-consuming thoughts. They went out late in the afternoon to eat and drink in a local wine bar returning late and collapsing into bed. In the morning, they were not as appreciative of the bell ringing as they normally were; both of them had serious hangovers. They didn't get up until the afternoon and decided it was best to travel to Cambridge by train rather than to drive as Richard was sure he would still be over the drink drive limit. They arrived back at Cambridge late afternoon and went their respective ways to prepare for the following week, after agreeing to meet on Wednesday to discuss the way forward on their task to change the world.

12

Monday passed by quite quickly for Richard as he got his teeth into some research, but Helen was having difficulty coming to terms with what she had learnt the day before. It continually came back into her mind, distracting her from her work. In addition to the new information she kept mulling over in her head, she was also thinking about the practical elements that she would need to deal with in this, such as the hypnosis and the responsibilities involved. She thought she would need to let her professional body know what she was going to be doing. Then she remembered the words of Sir Stuart, that for the time being no-one but the three of them could know. She couldn't wait until Wednesday. She called Richard and asked to meet that evening. Richard, agreed immediately, his research could wait, as he could sense she needed him. They met at his Cambridge flat a little after five. Richard had picked up some sushi and sandwiches from a delicatessen on the way and, after greeting her, offered Helen something to eat and drink. Helen, who seemed quite agitated, almost feverish, refused and said, "I couldn't wait until Wednesday. You know I want to review the file to the same point as you, so we are working together from the same base level. I'm quite worried by the responsibility of all of this and still have some questions and doubts, but they may be answered by the file to date."

Richard had emailed a copy of the latest version of the file to himself and he told his multimedia system to ready itself to play the file from the beginning. The system clicked and gently whined and the file started.

"Richard .... yes it is me and I am fine. Very dead in your understanding of the word but fine, please don't worry about me. You see I am in the next stage of being, beyond life, as we knew it, it does exist, the after-life. I know you will doubt that this is me but I assure you it is, I am with you, we all are everyone that has died, only not in being. It is as I thought here, time goes backwards so we know what is coming but time has little relevance as we can pass back and forth at will. We can also see your world; look out of the window, there is a small brown dog crossing the road without a care for the red car that is heading towards it. It won't hit the dog but it will be close".

Even though Sir Stuart had told her the file would no longer be interactive, Helen leapt up and looked out of the window but saw no dog and no car.

"This is where I said out loud how could the file know about that, but I didn't expect what came next," interjected Richard.

"I told you I can see your world." There was a pause. "Well, you remember the first two minutes of this recording, they were blank? That was me getting to know where I now am. Your two minutes was an eternity for me but not an unpleasant eternity in the context we sometimes used to use the word. With time running forwards or backwards, I know exactly what you are going to say and when, so my answers are pre-empting your questions. Even if you try to fool me by pausing, I know that too so I compensate in my text."

They listened to the file in silence, this time with belief as the file progressed. Later it continued, "You don't know much about hypnosis do you?" There was another pause, "That was a rehetorical question. I know you don't know, I've seen your lack of knowledge on the subject. Next week, at my funeral on Wednesday, you will meet a young woman who will change that. Her name is Helen Harrison and she is one of the country's leading authorities on hypnosis and hypnotherapy. When you meet, she will be pleased to discuss the concept with you and you must learn as much as you can from her. Do not at this stage mention what we have discussed here today. Also bear in mind that if you listen to this file again, it will not be interactive as the time for you has gone. You will still hear my voice but it would not make sense to anyone else as it will not be interactive and they are likely to be sceptical as a result. When you have learnt about hypnotherapy, come back and listen to the next part of this file." After another brief pause, the file continued, "Whenever you are ready. I will be here."
Richard cut in again, "At that I was concerned he would not be there again so I asked what if it was some time in the future and he answered," "No matter Richard, no matter, I will be here when you are ready. Remember, I have seen your life backwards so I will be here. Goodbye, my boy."

Helen and Richard continued to listen to the file all the way through including the part they had listened to the day before until they both heard the voice say, "There you are then, you are both now completely up to date and we are back live again. I suggest you now consider the matter together and then come back and speak to me again."
Helen replied first, "I have one more question at this stage."
"Fire away."
"As you will already know, my sister Jane cannot be hypnotised. Is there no way she can be part of this process, must she die at the normal age?" Helen said almost sobbing at the thought.
Sir Stuart responded in a soft caring voice, "I am afraid she cannot be part of it Helen, she will live a very long and fruitful life as you currently know it, but not in terms of the vastly extended life you will be able to offer to others. However," Sir Stuart continued but hesitated slightly as he knew this would be small comfort, "you have to think of this as being akin to finding a cure for some disease or other after a loved one has died, it's heartbreaking, but you are pleased for the ones that can be assisted in the future. This is similar, only this time the treatment will not work for all and that sometimes happens too with new drugs."
A tear rolled down Helen's face as she whimpered, "Yes, I understand."
Richard pulled her close to him to try to comfort her, but that just seemed to make things worse as she sobbed uncontrollably in his arms.
"Grandad," he said, "I will sign off now and speak to you again when we have had time to think, goodbye."

"Come back soon my boy and you too Helen, goodbye."
But she was past being able to speak.
"System off," Richard said and the click of the amplifier told him it was indeed now off.

Helen was heartbroken at this news, she had never dreamt that the inability of her sister to be hypnotised could have such devastating effect, in fact she had made fun of the fact in the past. Richard, continued to hold her until her tears subsided, she was not happy that Richard had to see her like this and she said, "Look at me, my eyes are all puffy now", as she got up and withdrew to the bathroom. When she came back, some considerable time later, she apologised to Richard, saying she felt foolish. Richard said that she was not and whilst she had been away he was beginning to wonder about who he knew that could not be hypnotised. He knew both his parents could be and he was now pleased they had been so embarrassing on the cruise where they went on stage, something he never expected. Helen and Richard continued to discuss this issue and in order to give Helen hope, said that perhaps when their IQ's were increased they would think of a way to overcome this. This didn't seem very likely to Helen as she thought Sir Stuart would have mentioned it. She considered that it was likely she would have to resign herself to it and as she considered this, she thought about her parents having to deal with the death of their daughter, reducing her to tears again. It was of course a long way off but somehow seemed very real now. Richard hugged her again in her time of despair. By now it was late and they both had had neither food nor drink for hours, but they couldn't really face eating so they had a nightcap and retired to bed. They held each other until they fell asleep.

Upon retiring the previous evening, Richard had forgotten to set the alarm but that mattered not as the next morning Helen was awake early and could not return to sleep as her mind was spinning, so she got up to make tea. When she returned to Richard, he had awoken too. He was lying in bed on his back with his hands clasped behind his head.

"I think I'll go to the gym this morning," he said, "I've been neglecting my training recently and it's not long now until the Games, you know." He was referring to the 2012 Olympic Games, where his sport was being held at Eton Dorney near Windsor, in August. Although he was very fit anyway, he realised he still had a great deal of work to do on his fitness before then. Helen, also a keen sportswoman, but not of Olympic standard, thought it would be good to go to the gym early before going to work, thinking it might clear her head.

"Me too," she agreed, suddenly finding something to focus upon, "I'll come with you."

They drank their tea, dressed and left together to go to the Riversedge Club where they were both members, although they had never run into each other there in the past due to differing timetables.

After training, which they did together to spur each other on, they showered and changed for work before having an orange juice and a cappuccino at the bar. Both felt quite invigorated and ready for the day. As they parted, Richard kissed Helen tenderly and for the first time she told him she loved him. Somewhat taken

aback, Richard replied rather bashfully, "I love you too." They kissed again and started to walk away from each other when Richard turned and shouted, "Don't forget lunch with my parents on Easter Sunday."
"I hope I see you before then," she teased.
"Of course," he replied, smiling, "see you tomorrow night as we originally planned."

On the Wednesday when they met they decided not to discuss SHINE but instead went to the Cambridge Arts Picture House, opposite the University, to the film festival where a special showing of the *Life and Times of Marlene Dietrich*, was on, a film that Helen was particularly keen to see as Jane had recommended it. Helen highly rated her sister's approval as she always liked the films and theatre that Jane suggested. Richard however, was not so enthused, but said nothing. He was more interested in the Thai restaurant just along the road from the cinema where they ate after seeing the early showing of the film. In the event, Richard did enjoy the film and was pleased he had seen it which they discussed at length over dinner with a few of his friends they bumped into at the Thai. They left the restaurant to walk the few hundred metres to Richard's flat where Helen stayed the night. By now she had a wardrobe not only at her house, but also at the Cambridge flat and some clothes at St. John's Wood. This pleased her as it gave her the perfect excuse, not that she needed one, to go out shopping for clothes for each location. Richard hated shopping for clothes, which showed by the way he dressed, but Helen had plans to change that and by now he knew better than to object when she was in retail therapy mode.

As they retired for the night, they had good intentions of going to the gym before work in the morning again but in the event, they had slightly overdone it in the restaurant so decided to sleep in instead until the last minute before they both had to leave for work. Parting company, they agreed to meet on Good Friday at the gym before they got down to business on the development of SHINE and its activities.

13

The Gym was relatively empty early on Friday morning with most people having gone away for the weekend; so they rattled through their programmes and headed off for breakfast in a local café. It was not the healthiest of meals, but they figured that they had earned it after their workout and that made it all the tastier. They were both in good spirits and they joked and laughed as they had their breakfast. Their mood began to change however, as they walked back to Richard's flat to get down to some serious discussion about the daunting task they had been given. Back at the flat, Richard turned the radio on before he settled down on the sofa. Helen could have done without the background noise, but instead asked if Richard could turn it down a bit, which he did. For a while they both sat there thinking, feeling overwhelmed by the task at hand. They both started to talk at once. Richard said, "I think we should..." just as Helen said, "If we start with..." This made them laugh, which broke the tension a bit and Richard said, "What were you going to say?"

"If we start with a plan of what we need to discuss, an agenda if you like, that might focus us on the important

issues which we can then prioritise. What were you going to say?"
"I was going to say the same. I think we should start with a list of items we need to deal with then prioritise the main concerns."
"Agreed." said Helen. "Do you have a large piece of paper and some coloured pens?"
Richard walked to his study and brought back a roll of lining wallpaper and some coloured highlighter pens. He spread the paper over the coffee table securing it with sticky tape at the corners to prevent it from curling up. They both sat on the floor next to the table on the same side and Richard wrote at the top in the middle as a heading 'SHINE' in a dark green pen.
"My favourite colour," he said.
"I know," Helen replied, smiling at his surprise that she knew.
They decided to brainstorm to get the issues down on paper, not worrying about the categories. They could re-write those later on another sheet, except that Richard split the paper in two columns by drawing a line vertically down from the title with the heading 'IQ ENHANCEMENT' on the left side and 'LONGEVITY' on the other. Helen picked up the red pen and wrote 'hypnosis and hypnotherapy' straddling both columns.
"That is the key to all of this, the cornerstone," she said.
Richard nodded in agreement. They both sat back for a moment and looked at the sheet before continuing further. Richard said, "I think we should say the heading first then discuss where it should go, don't you?"
"Yes okay," she replied, "but what about 'afterlife'?"

"We leave that out for the time being," replied Richard. "My grandfather thought it best for now at least until the IQ enhancement and more particularly the IQ building period has had a chance to kick in."
"There's the first entry, IQ building period, on the left hand side." Helen said writing it down in blue pen. "Moral issues are another," she continued.
"That should be on both sides," Richard suggested.
Helen wrote moral issues in the middle under hypnosis and hypnotherapy.

Soon they had raised and categorised many issues on the paper and had ceased to make any sensible additions to the list for several minutes, whereupon Richard said, "I think we've dried up, perhaps that will do for now. Let's see, what have we got? Under 'IQ enhancement' we have:

- IQ Building Period
- Base Alteration
- Conversion Process
- Sub-Hypnosis
- Further Hypnotherapists
- Vetting Process
- Brain Training
- SHINE
- Scepticism
- Fear
- The First Converts
- DNA Binary
- Location
- Funding
- Government

- Control and Prevention of Corruption
- Professional Bodies
- Failure or Non-ability to Participate
- Agreement to Participate
- Refusal to Participate
- The Terminally Ill
- Misuse of power
- The Latent Brain
- Brain Reserve

Helen followed up with “and under ‘Longevity’, other than some of those issues already raised in column one that overlap, we have:

- Timing after IQ Enhancement
- The Process
- Agreement to Participate
- Refusal to Participate
- Failure or Non-ability to Participate
- Population Explosion
- Potential Famine
- Mismatched Ageing
- Mortality

“Do you suppose that’s everything?” Helen asked.
“There is one more thing,” said Richard.
“What’s that?”
“It’s your willingness to be involved in this, bearing in mind that Jane cannot be included in either programme.”
“I’ve thought that through Richard and I cannot allow it to stand in the way of this. It’s bigger than my family or me and it will happen in any event so I would rather be

involved at the sharp end than not at all. I will just have to enjoy her life for the next sixty or seventy years and hopefully the increased IQ of others can come up with some drugs or techniques to enhance and improve her life naturally, after all there was the woman who lived to 122. Regarding IQ, I understand that there is currently already research into implanting memory chips into the skull of a person that will vastly improve their memory and this will have an effect on their IQ so there may be ways to help those who cannot take part. So," she drew breath, "count me in."

Both were pleased with their efforts and after rewriting the order of the lists, they decided to call it a day as they were both mentally drained. They would recommence again tomorrow. They settled down to watch TV leaving the new list still taped to the coffee table. In the morning, after the usual ablutions, Richard switched the system on to watch breakfast TV, or at least listen to it as he prepared, and they ate, breakfast. Helen and Richard discussed their efforts the night before and agreed that they should recommence their work on SHINE Therapy whilst it was fresh in their memories, but before possibly going off at a tangent, Richard suggested they consult his grandfather on the progress they had made thus far.
As the system was already switched on Richard commanded "System, play the file from where it left off."
The voice was almost instant, "Good morning to you both."
"Good morning," they replied together.

Richard continued immediately, wasting no time with niceties, "As you will know, we have prepared a list of priorities relating to SHINE Therapy and we want to run it past you in case we have missed anything."
Helen took over, reading out their list that was now categorised into similar items and prioritised.

As she finished, Sir Stuart said, "Seems very comprehensive, well done; but just one small point for you Helen before we go any further. I wanted you to make your decision to go forward on the basis of your sister not being able to be part of the programme. However, as you rightly determined, there will be ways of assisting her in her natural life that will improve her IQ and lifespan, not as it will be for you, but it will be vastly different to what currently happens. She will live twice as long as the current norm." Helen, seizing upon that hope said, "Thank you for telling me, knowing that makes me feel much happier about her future." She looked at Richard who was smiling at her sympathetically.
"Right," Sir Stuart continued, "back to your list."
They both sat back waiting for the pearls of wisdom to emanate from Richard's grandfather. "Your list is very comprehensive, but there are a couple of points you may wish to consider." They listened intently.
"First, you have not given any thought to the level of IQ that can be achieved and that will be the first question people will ask. However, the answer is quite simple really. Currently, excluding profound mental retardation, severe, moderate and mild MR, all of which will be eradicated by DNA alteration, IQ's range from 'normal dull' at 80- 90 to 'very superior' at over 130.

Beyond that, there are people such as yourselves with IQ's of much higher than that, 162, for Richard and 155, for you Helen. As I have told you, when you are 'base-altered' it will give you 80% more of your conscious brain volume for general use so your capacity will be nine fold, retaining a further 10% for survival needs. Thus your Intelligence Quotient will be substantially more powerful than it is now. There are a number of factors that will affect just how much of a gain an individual will receive but essentially the higher an IQ before enhancement, the greater the potential increase. It will work on the basis of a sliding scale. You Richard will have a factor of 1.8 applied to your IQ taking it to 292, and Helen, you will have a factor of 1.76 making your new IQ 272."

"That's a massive increase," Richard said, in a somewhat surprised fashion as he lifted his hands to clasp his head.

"Exactly so Richard," His grandfather responded, "Exactly so."

Richard smiled at the thought of so much brain power, what could he achieve with it he wondered as he drifted off for a moment. Helen too was deep in thought at the consequences of such an improvement in her brainpower; she was wondering how it would feel emotionally. Sir Stuart gave them some time to reflect on this, saying nothing until they were quite ready to take in some more information. They both realised that he was silent, as together they looked towards the multimedia system thinking something had happened to it.

"Next," Sir Stuart said breaking the silence, "relating to longer life, you have not considered the implications of potential boredom."
"Boredom?" Richard interrupted, "how so, what do you mean?"
"Well," his grandfather carried on, "people will live for up to ten times as long as they do now. However, not everyone is as happy with their lot as you two are; some people hate their work and the thought of doing the same thing for hundreds of years will not please them at all. You must come up with a programme of development for those that want a change, as most of you will, at least five if not more times in your extended lives. To fail in this will have devastating consequences with a massive increase in suicide."
Neither of them had given this any attention whatsoever, indeed it had not even entered their heads. "But not everyone can have top echelon careers, what about the service industries, who will still want to do that when they have superior brain power?" Helen asked, annoyed with herself that she had missed this important aspect of human behaviour.
Sir Stuart explained, "As I have told you, there will still be a differential between the top and the bottom as there is now, however, everyone, even those with the lowest IQ's will be more than capable of achieving anything they want to in terms of anyone's current achievements. Therefore, you must set rules. Some of the more menial tasks will disappear of course with the innovations and inventions that the new 'base altered' human race will develop. However, some of the need will remain, so employment must be categorised into different levels and each person who wants to go

through SHINE Therapy must agree to undertake a period of time in the service industries, trades or to do manual labour."

"Will people agree to that?" Helen asked.

"You have already discussed limiting the number of children people can have, will they agree to that?" Stuart offered and to answer his question before anyone had time to reply he continued, "of course they will, there is always give and take in any situation and people will realise the sense in the restrictions, particularly after base-alteration. However, inextricably linked with that is the issue of fidelity. Many marriages do not make it now with a maximum of only seventy years together. Do you suppose many will make it last hundreds of years? Greater intelligence will help, but you need to consider this too."

Helen was now even more annoyed with herself that she had missed this issue too.

Stuart continued, "Now, I will leave you to work your way through your list, we can speak again when you are ready."

Helen and Richard spent the rest of the day debating the issues that they and Stuart had proposed. By evening, exhausted, they became aware that again they had not eaten all day. After yet another delivery meal they retired to bed to be fresh for their visit to Richard's parents the following day. Helen was not nearly as traumatised at the prospect of meeting Richard's parents as Richard had been at meeting hers; but nevertheless she wanted to make a good impression so took quite a time to make herself ready. Richard was a little apprehensive at the idea of his parents meeting

Helen and by taking her time getting ready she was not helping his nerves. However, he said nothing as she continued to titivate herself in readiness for the meeting. Richard tried to remain calm by absorbing himself in the Sunday papers which he read as he lay on the floor of the lounge, propping his chin on his hands with his elbows on the floor.

"You can't be comfortable like that," Helen observed as she walked into the room. Richard looked round, "Yes, I'm ..." He stopped mid-sentence. Helen looked stunning; he was speechless initially but then managed a, "You look beautiful." in a sighing voice that said it all.

"Thank-you," she replied, "but you need a clothes brush; you've managed to pick up every bit of fluff from the carpet on your suit."

"Oh, damn," he responded, as he rushed for the drawer where the clothes brush lived. She followed him, took the brush and brushed him down, laughing as she did so. When they finally left it was a little after 1:30 p.m. and he was tempted to phone his mum to say they were on their way, but resisted, thinking they should make it. Sunday lunch was always at 2.00 p.m. promptly and look out anyone who was late.

It was not far to his parents and a nice walk in the Easter sunshine if a little cold. Richard's father was in the front garden as they arrived.

"Hello son." he said as they reached the gate.

"Hello Dad, this is Helen," Richard blustered as he shook his father's hand warmly.

"I thought it might be," he returned sarcastically, "Hello Helen, good to meet you at last, I'm James."

He glanced at Richard and the 'at last' was heavily enunciated. Richard thought that a little unnecessary

but ignored it. "Let's go in," James continued, "lead the way Richard, your mother will be almost ready by now, you're just in time."
Helen was led through to the Kitchen by Richard where Penny was just finalising lunch. "Hello Mum", said Richard, "how are you?"
"I'm fine thank you Darling, how are you? I've seen little of you recently," she said drying her hands on a tea towel before embracing him.
"I've been busy with Helen. Errr, I mean Helen and I have been busy. Errr, we've been working on a project together."
His embarrassment was obvious to his mother and to Helen. In an effort to ease his pain, Helen stepped forward and said, "Hello Mrs. Harper, I've heard so much about you."
"Oh, call me Penny, please," she replied trying not to laugh at her son's embarrassment. "Richard has told me you're a leading hypnotherapist," Penny continued.
"Yes, but I'm not so sure about the 'leading' part sometimes; it's fraught with critics who continue to decry the practice," said Helen as they walked together into the dining room where everything was set out precisely on the table.
"Not for long though," said Richard rather indiscreetly, but no one picked up on it except Helen who gave him a sideways glance.
The meal went well and they were all getting along famously. Richard by now was more relaxed and thought it was about time he got his own back on his dad for the 'at last' comment in the garden when they arrived. He chirped up "So Dad, why do you no longer use the name Alex?"

James jaw dropped. He looked at his wife in surprise who exclaimed, "Goodness, I've not heard anyone call you that for thirty years. How did you find that out Richard?"

"So it is true then, Alex," Richard said. He and Helen laughed at his parents' surprise and proceeded to explain that Helen's father was at school with James. After the usual, 'it's a small world' expressions James asked Helen to arrange for him and her father to meet sometime which she agreed to do saying, "Perhaps you and Dad can have a beer together sometime."

"Yes, that would be nice, I'm partial to the odd beer," said James, smiling.

"The odd beer!" exclaimed Penny. They all laughed. With the meal finished, Helen thanked Penny, complimenting her on her culinary skills and asked if she could help with the clearing up. Penny thanked her, but told her to go with Richard to the lounge and that she and 'Alex' would do it. Helen and Richard retired to the lounge and as they sipped their coffee they reflected on how the world in future might not be so small; not with the programme they had in mind. It wasn't long before Richard's parents came into the room where they settled down just in time to watch the downhill skiing from Innsbruck. Skiing, they had realised over lunch was a shared passion. As always, Britain didn't even come close, but they all enjoyed the competition anyway and after Ski Sunday had finished, Richard and Helen decided it was time to leave to return to his flat. On the way, Helen thought she should pop in to see her parents briefly as she had not been home for a few days and they would be wondering where she was, or perhaps not, now that they had met

Richard. Her parents were of course very pleased to see them both, but were about to leave to go out for a late dinner with friends so Richard and Helen stayed only for a few minutes before returning to Richard's flat where they settled down to watch some TV before retiring early. They had a big day ahead of them continuing with their organisation of the SHINE Therapy Centres. They were however resolute that before they started the work, they would clear their minds by going to the gym in the morning.

14

They were awake long before the campanologists at the local Church started their Easter Monday routine. Richard switched on the multimedia system so he could hear the news as he prepared his sports kit. He couldn't find his training shoes and was fiddling around not really making any progress on getting himself out the door. Helen on the other hand was already prepared and said to him, "Come on slowcoach, it will be lunchtime before you're ready."
At that very instant Richard found his training shoes under the bed, stuffed them into his sports bag and ran through the hallway to the front door. He then darted into the lounge and hit a button on the multimedia system to turn it off and ran back to the front door where Helen was waiting with a look on her face that said, 'You are a nutcase'.
"You ready now?" she said mockingly.
"Yes, let's go." Richard responded smacking her playfully on the bum as he passed her.
The gym session was over before they knew it and again there were very few members in that morning. They had breakfast at the gym and afterwards returned to

the flat mid-morning and got down to some serious thinking.
Being Easter Monday, there was an extended bell ringing that went on for over half-an-hour. This did not best please Richard as it was ruining his concentration; nevertheless they persevered through the noise, closing the windows they had opened to ensure a constant supply of fresh air to aid their thought processes.

By now, they were both utterly convinced that what they had been chosen to do was within their capabilities and what wasn't as yet, they firmly believed would be, after they were base-altered. Nonetheless they were somewhat worried by the prospect of the base alteration and decided to tackle that subject first. They knew from Sir Stuart that Helen would have to be the first to undergo the treatment. She could hypnotise herself and then Sir Stuart could take over to take her to the sub-hypnosis level where he could guide her to altering her own DNA. Richard could then go second when Helen had learnt DNA binary that Sir Stuart had told them should not take too long. That was all very well they thought, but how could they move on from there. Unless Richard learnt hypnosis, they had no male to hypnotise the females at the sub-hypnosis level, other than Sir Stuart of course, but his part was not to be made public yet so it could not be him except in Helen's case. Richard would of course be able to learn to be a hypnotherapist relatively easily with his superior intellect, but he had other issues to deal with such as the finances and convincing governments to go with the programme. No, they needed to confide in a third person, a man who was already a hypnotherapist and

someone they could trust. He would not be told about Sir Stuart, which would remain their secret.
Helen though for a moment or two, then she said, "I have it, I have the answer. Do you remember when I went to Helsinki?"
Richard nodded affirmatively. "Well, one of the speakers, a German, Hans Groeber, was pushing the boundaries of the science of hypnosis. His subject had not been well received by the conference delegates, but what he said now makes perfect sense to me. He is of the opinion, and it was only a theory of his at that time, that there was a more fundamental use for hypnosis than curing phobias and helping people stop smoking et cetera and he was researching it further. He was looking for a partner to assist him, but there were no takers at the time. He is a brilliant hypnotherapist, but sometimes misunderstood as he constantly tries to push the boundaries."
"Just what the doctor ordered then," said Richard a little flippantly, "let's contact him immediately."
"Yes Richard, just what the doctor ordered, he is precisely the right man for the job," said his grandfather's voice.
They both jumped, startled, how could they be hearing this? The system was off. Richard slowly turned around expecting his grandfather to be sitting in his wheelchair; after all it was Easter, perhaps he had resurrected. Nothing could surprise him now, but no one was there; Richard leapt up and crossed to the multimedia system. It was on. He realised that he must have switched it to 'play the file' earlier when he hit the buttons as he rushed out of the flat to go to the gym and had not switched it off as he had thought.

"Don't do that!" he called out to his grandfather, "I thought you were back from the dead."
"Not possible I'm afraid," said his grandfather, "no one can or will be able to do that."
"There will be a lot of disappointed cryogenics then," said Richard, thinking quickly.
"No, they may be saddened that they cannot go back, but they will be happy that there is an after-life and that they will see their loved ones again in any event," came the reply.
"Anyway, I digress. I can't believe I've wasted so much of the file time."
"No you haven't Richard," said his grandfather "there was nothing on the file for the 2 hours you were away; you forget, I knew you were going to leave the system on."
"Of course," said Richard relieved.
Helen, who had now regained her composure, asked, "So you agree that Hans is the one we should contact?"
"Yes," said Sir Stuart, "and he will readily agree."
"Grandad, we don't really have any questions for you at present so we shall close your file now and speak later if that's okay?"
"That's fine Richard, that's just fine by me, goodbye."
"Goodbye," they both said together and Richard added, "system off."
"Actually, Richard, I did have a question, but I suppose you and I should discuss it between ourselves first?"
"Oh yes, what is that?"
"Well, despite limiting families to two children, I'm worried that there will still be a population explosion eventually as time passes because there will be many

more people living at the same time on what is already an overpopulated planet."

"Yes and no," Richard responded not really helping Helen initially, and then he continued. "Yes, there will be many more people, approximately ten times as many, but that will be a gradual process over the next six or seven hundred years giving man time to deal with the issues that arise, indeed for the next generation or so, not much will change in terms of population explosion and the potential for famine, so we have time to tackle this."

"And the no?" Helen said, probing further.

"The planet is not overused. It may be at present with our current technology and farming methods, but more than two-thirds is sea and of the land, more than a third of that is desert, so you see, we currently use very little of the space available, about twenty per cent or so. I predict that within a few years of the SHINE Therapy increasing IQ, we will have a satellite system in place that can reflect the sun away from the deserts, creating huge shaded but warm areas, onto other areas that currently cannot be used for either farming or for man's habitation," Richard continued with Helen looking on in amazement at his vision.

"The seas can be built upon with massive structures similar to oil rig platforms, but supporting new lands well above the water line." He hesitated to think, Helen didn't intervene, and then he continued, "Did you know that if you were to take a globe of the earth and trace onto paper the outline of the main continents, cut those out and invert them so that north was south, they would all fit into the existing sea areas with ease? That way we can double the land mass and with the sun deflector system also, we can make so much more of the existing land available and use areas of new land where formerly only deserts could flourish."

"Wow," exclaimed Helen absolutely blown away by his predictions. "Do you really believe that Richard?"

"Yes, firmly, and what's more it will not be long before we crack nuclear fusion after our IQ upgrade and you will not believe the difference that will make to us all. That will also assist us to travel quickly and more safely to other planets and space stations where further colonies can be established."

Helen was a little sceptical, but she thought, Richard was the scientist and he seemed so confident in his abilities that she decided to accept what he said, at least for now.

One issue that bothered Helen was the ozone layer and how all of this would affect an issue already close to her heart, global warming. Also, what about the Gulf Stream and other ocean currents? Would millions of columns into the seas to support new lands not affect that? She was about to ask Richard who was deep in thought and as if by telepathy he started to answer her questions.

"With our vastly improved brain capacity and understanding, we will be able to prevent any further global warming, perhaps even reverse it."

He said this with glazed eyes that were showing by now he was almost in a trance. Helen recognised it as a form of self-hypnosis and let him carry on.

"Doubtless we will discover new materials far stronger than those which exist now that will be able to span further and support more load with shapes that will not

affect the environment, perhaps even mesh with nature. New seafood will come from the deeper seas that are currently unexploited with future exploration being made possible by the same materials. Mini climates can be created by man where and when he wants them, twenty-four hours a day sunshine to increase plant and food growth. I can see it all now, it will be incredible," he exclaimed excitedly.
Helen, who until then sat quietly listening to him said, "Richard, I think I am just beginning to realise the implications of this, the responsibility that will rest with us and that the hypnosis is just a very small, but important part of the entire change. As you said, a new Genesis. A complete and absolute change to life as we know it and we must be very careful to keep control, as it could so easily be used irresponsibly in the wrong hands. We need to ensure that does not happen, Richard, we need to plan this very carefully, very carefully indeed."

They spent the rest of that day discussing the enlistment of Hans Groeber and what they should and should not tell him about the process. Recognising that he was a highly intelligent man, it would be difficult to explain it to him without giving him the full picture of DNA binary. They decided to wait until they were both base-altered to the IQ enhancement stage before going further with this as they figured it would be to their advantage. They also decided that in order that family, friends and colleagues would not think it odd that they were so absorbed in this that they could not even work, they would keep their planning to evenings and weekends. They agreed that Helen should go through the base-alteration the following weekend. The week went very slowly for both of them despite being a four-day week. They met at the gym twice and Helen went out with some girlfriends on the Friday night. However, she found it very difficult to concentrate and on more than one occasion she was asked if she was all right. She said she was, but her friends didn't believe her, so she said she was seeing Richard the next day to sort a few things out which took the focus away from her as her friends realised she didn't want to talk about it. In truth, she was wondering how the increased IQ would affect her relationships with her friends until they too were base-altered which might be some time away due to the enormity of the task. She left early and went home to bed but not before calling Richard to say she would be round at nine. During the call, Richard told Helen that he had worked during the week in his research laboratory, but he too had had other things on his mind. He couldn't help thinking that the complex research formulas upon which he was working this week would be simple tasks in a few weeks. That prospect sapped the little incentive to work that he did have; he hated wasting time. He told her that although she was going first, he still felt like a condemned man. What would it feel like? Would they still feel positive about the process for the entire human race? Helen too was worried and was as supportive as the telephone would permit. She suggested that perhaps she should go to him. He refused, suggesting she should get a good night's sleep, something that in the event evaded them both. He lay there all night tossing and turning. However, one thing he was sure of now was there was no going back.

He had so many questions in his head but he decided to save them for his grandfather the following morning when Helen would be there too. His main concern was that Helen was going first, the guinea pig. He didn't like that idea, he wanted to be first, but he knew that was impossible.

15

Helen was prompt, arriving at exactly nine o'clock. Richard was already up and dressed and had even managed a little breakfast. Helen had eaten before leaving home, her mother had insisted, but she had a cup of Richard's cappuccino, which by now she was rather partial to.

With their coffees next to them, the two settled in the lounge and Richard commanded the system to turn on and to play the file from where it last left off. It hummed into action, "Good morning both," said the voice of his grandfather, "I trust you are well."

"You know we are not," said Richard rather tersely, still suffering from lack of sleep.

"Well, Richard," his grandfather continued, "not for much longer. When you are base-altered, your brain will require much less rest, only your body will require time to recuperate but four hours in a twenty-four hour period will suffice you in the future."

This was news to Richard and Helen and had not been discussed before. Nevertheless, he would look forward to that, but it was not yet the case thought Richard as he yawned.

Helen then asked her various questions and sought solace with respect to her doubts and Sir Stuart gave her a detailed explanation that satisfied even her inquisitive nature. Her final question, "What of our future, our relationships?" which was seeking reassurance with regard to her relationships with other people before they were base-altered, was met with an overview of how their lives would pan out and to the astonishment of them both Sir Stuart predicted that they would marry. It was not that they might marry that was the shock; they both knew that by now, but that they should hear it predicted as a certainty. They looked at each other longingly wishing that they were alone, but Sir Stuart merely said knowingly, "Come on you two, work to be done, there's time for that later."
Helen blushed and Richard realised that was the first time he had seen her embarrassed, it showed another side to her that he had not seen and made him realise just how deeply in love he was with her.

Never needing to be told twice, Helen set up the area for her self-hypnosis ready for Sir Stuart to take over. She lay on the sofa and started the tape of her colleague that was going to hypnotise her. Richard was beside himself, there was nothing he could do but watch. The tape began.
"If you are comfortable Helen we shall begin," said the voice of Helen's colleague whose tape she had used on several occasions before to self-hypnotise.
"Helen, I want you to relax fully, make yourself completely at ease and close your eyes. That's it, be completely at ease and relaxed, close your eyes... permit your mind to be free and to drift anywhere it

cares to go, anywhere your mind would feel safe for you to be... and, be aware of your muscles, allow them to go limp and loose, your feet and ankles want to relax, let them relax, that's it, let them relax, ... to become limp. Allow your calves to go too, let them be loose and fully relaxed, your knees and thighs, let your thighs relax, allow them to be loose too, that's it."

As the voice continued, Richard could see Helen's body almost melting into the sofa with relaxation. The voice continued to give instructions to Helen telling her to relax fully all parts of her body from feet to head, telling her that she should go down deeper and deeper and let her body go, feeling drowsier and drowsier, to relax completely. Before long she was completely under in one of the deepest level of hypnotic state she had ever been to. The room fell silent. Richard was now on the edge of his seat looking at Helen in her trance then looking at the sound system, then back to Helen. All of a sudden, his grandfather said "Helen, this is now Stuart, I want to talk to your base consciousness, is that acceptable to you?"

Helen nodded in agreement and softly said, "Yes".

"I want your base consciousness to take me to your DNA strands where I will guide you to alter just one part of your DNA, to allow you to access the area of your brain that currently you cannot access to give you eighty percent more brain function. Is that acceptable to you?"

Again Helen nodded and softly said, "Yes".

"Take me to your DNA strands, ... are you there yet?" his grandfather continued. Again she nodded and said yes in agreement.

At this point Richard's grandfather started talking what sounded like gibberish to Richard. "Ips, dol, lup, tev, raq, wiv, lud, qem, aum, tew, lam." He continued, "Snu, tav, yif, kep." He stopped talking for a few moments then said, "Helen, I am now going to bring you to a full waking state, you will be alert and every part of you will return to the here and now. You will feel completely normal, all sensations will be with you. I will now count from one to ten. By the count of eight your eyes will open, fully and easily and by the count of ten you will be completely alert. You will feel fine, refreshed and energised," he spoke faster now "one, two, three, more aware, four, five, six, more alert," and still faster "seven, eight, eyes fully open, nine, ten fully awake back in the here and now."

Helen opened her eyes, smiled and said, "Hello, I'm back" to the great relief of Richard.

"Well," he said, "How does it feel?" "I have an unbelievable awareness Richard. There is an overwhelming feeling of a desire to learn."

She sat up and started talking to Sir Stuart about the topics she and Richard had established relating to SHINE Therapy. Richard was amazed at the clarity of her thought process. However, the speed of delivery of her words was ever increasing, it sounded like a recording being played at fast forward speed. Richard could not keep up so he took the digital dictating device that Helen had been using to self hypnotise and set it to record. He could slow it down later, if indeed they were speaking English. The pace of the discussion was electric then suddenly it was over. Helen flopped into the sofa, unconscious. Richard ran to her and taking her in his arms said, "Helen, Helen, what's the matter?"

"It's okay my boy, she is merely sleeping," said his grandfather, "clearly it was all too much for her, she has used up all the energy that her old brain power would permit. She will be fine after a short sleep. Switch me off until then."

And short it was, she awoke after only thirty minutes and was on top of the world again and restarted the file.

"How long for me to learn DNA binary Stuart?" she said.

"About half-an-hour," came the reply. "Longer to fully brain-train you though; that will be about a month as I have told you."

"Let's get started then; I can't take having a man who is less intelligent than me around," she said, laughing.

Richard didn't see the funny side and said "Are you sure you are up to it?"

"Absolutely."

Richard felt redundant so decided to go off and get them some food. He went to the local Fresco Express supermarket to pick up something for later, although when he got there he was not exactly concentrating, so instead of getting one full meal he got several parts of a meal, they would have to make do, he wanted to get back.

When he got back Helen hugged him and said: "Your turn."

"What, you have mastered it already, DNA binary I mean?"

"Fluent," came the reply from Stuart. So without much protest, Richard was made ready and within twenty minutes he too was base-altered with Stuart taking him through the first level and Helen dealing with the base alteration, which she handled as though she had been practising it for years.

"Well done," said Stuart as Richard awoke. "I suggest you get some sleep like Helen did before you go much further today."

"Yes, I think I overdid it," said Helen, "I was so excited."

Richard in the meantime had picked up his Rubik Cube, the solution to which had always evaded him despite his high IQ. Within ten seconds of frantic twisting and clicking he had solved it. He put it down, beaming from ear to ear. He moved to Helen, hugged her and kissed her warmly.

"I don't care if you can see this Grandad; I love her, which, amongst other things, is so vivid now."

The old man chuckled.

Richard said, "Talk to you later Grandad," as he commanded the system off.

"Goodbye both." The old man replied.

They took each other in their arms and made passionate love in front of the fire in the lounge before both dropping off to sleep. It had been an extremely tiring day. However, they were amazed to be awake again only a short period later. In fact they had only been asleep for an hour but they were now fully awake and they both felt ready for anything. After a catch up on what Helen had been discussing with Sir Stuart earlier, they decided to eat and had a good laugh together when Helen saw what Richard had bought. She managed to cobble something together using what he had bought that hit the spot though, as they were both ravenous. Both of them were discussing the clarity with which they could now see things. Issues that had seemed to evade them before were now crystal clear and it did not take long for them to work their way through the priority list they had created for setting up SHINE Therapy Centres, refining it to a sharp focus as they did so. They also decided to contact Hans Groeber the next day, but before they did, they had the idea it would be good if they learned to speak German; after all it should only take them a few hours or so. They were both so happy with their new abilities and Helen was particularly pleased that it did not seem to alter the way in which she considered her various relationships, although the acid test would be when she met her friends again. As for Richard, he just kept looking at the Rubik Cube whilst smiling broadly.

In the morning, after a quick trip to a local bookshop to pick up 'Teach Yourself German' and an English/German translation book they set about learning the new language. As they had predicted, it didn't take long and for the rest of the morning they only spoke in German to each other, so by the time they were ready to videophone Hans, they were both fluent and without a hint of an English accent.

However, one thing was bothering Richard and that was the number of rules that he felt it would be necessary to impose on the new way of life and that that might cause disquiet for others. He raised the point with Helen who had also been thinking about that, but her response was simply, "Don't you suppose Moses thought the same when he came back with the Commandments?"

"Interesting," Richard said, "that was what I compared this to when I was talking to my grandfather before you knew about this, do you remember?"
"Yes," she replied, "I remember everything, remember, particularly now," she teased, but followed up with, "we are only the messengers, not dictators and people will have a choice." Richard nodded in agreement and switched the system on ready for the video link to Hans.

The system hummed quietly whilst they made themselves comfortable in front of the camera above the system's flat screen. Helen dialled the number for Hans and waited the few moments for him to answer. It was a little after four in the afternoon for them so just after five for Hans. Hans answered the phone in his best English accent when he saw Helen on his screen. "Hello Helen, how are you my dear?" Making slight fun of Helen's refined English accent. He was however completely astonished by her fluent German response "Hello, Hans, I am well thank you."
After regaining his composure but still looking a little shocked, Hans replied in his more usual English, "I didn't know you can speak German, when do you learn?"
"Yes" she continued in a perfect German accent, "I will come back to that. Hans, I would like you to meet my boyfriend Richard Harper."
"Hello Richard, I've hear lot about you." Hans continued in his imperfect English.
"Hello, Hans." Richard also spoke in perfect German. "I have heard a lot about you too, from Helen. You do some good work in hypnotherapy and it is that which we urgently need to discuss with you, but it must be face to face, not over the videophone."

Reverting to German and in answer to Richard's direct approach, intrigued, Hans told them that he would be in London later that week and would be pleased to meet then. Helen asked Hans where he would be staying and he replied that as yet he had not booked anywhere. Richard looked at Helen and said, "Good, you can stay with us, if that's okay with you Hans?"

"Ja, ja, that would be good, thank you," Hans said, pleased at the thought of not needing to book a hotel.

"I will email you details of how to get to St John's Wood where the flat is," said Helen. "Okay, great, I meet with you both Thursday then, Ja?" replied Hans.

"Yes, see you then," Richard and Helen said together, "Bye."

The link closed and Richard instructed the system to change to background music as Helen went off to the toilet. When she came back Richard was getting ready to go to the gym.

"Are you going to come?" he asked.

"Yes, I think I will," she said. "otherwise my brain just keeps on thinking. It's weird, isn't it?"

"Yes." Richard replied, not waiting for, or needing, further explanation. He knew just how she was thinking. "It is weird, but I'm sure we will get used to it."

Helen quickly prepared her bag and they set off to the gym where they had a good workout that didn't enable them to detach themselves in the way it had in the past, but it did make them both feel good and at least tired them physically, if not mentally.

Over the next few days, they discussed the set up of SHINE and with the guidance of his grandfather, Richard looked into investments to return him funding for the new centres. London was to be the first centre, but they didn't want to jump the gun. They could not open it until governments knew of the plan. Richard and Helen could however make a decision as to where and how big the centre should be, but on this there was a bit of a dilemma as it was to be the flagship centre but, by the same token, they didn't want it to be too brash. After some rapid deliberation, they decided to take space in the National Hospital for Neurology and Neurosurgery at Queen Square in London. In that way they could have the prestige of the name of one of the world's best-known hospitals, but the anonymity of their own space within it to carry out their work.

Richard quickly mastered the shares and futures markets and with the assistance of his grandfather he set about investing. Not wanting to attract attention to himself he initially placed small amounts of his grandfather's inheritance in steadily growing funds that his grandfather had told him were good. His knowledge of the future enabled him to know precisely when to get out of the shares before they turned. He also bought into some shares that he knew would lose money in order that he would not attract attention as a winner only.

His grandfather directed Richard to another, and previously undetected, file that he had hidden in the System File folder in his computer. Stuart had written this file just after the speech file that Richard and Helen were listening to. It had such an obscure name that no-one would have given it a second thought even if they had looked at it.

Within this file was a list of all the dates for the next 200 years when certain share values would surge and that Richard should invest in to maximise his share profits. Richard carefully backed up the file and put a copy away for safe keeping with the backup of the other file of his grandfather. If this were to fall into the wrong hands it would be disastrous.

All of this was taking quite some time, however, as Richard did not need so much sleep now, time was something he had plenty of. With the vast processing power that he now commanded, his research took far less time than it did before. All he had to do was be careful that he did not solve research programmes too quickly in front of others and raise suspicion. 'A couple of good ideas a week should be enough', he thought.

By contrast, Helen, who was still working at her hypnotherapy consultancy practice, was itching to move forward. Never known for her patience; she wanted to change the world immediately and Thursday's meeting with Hans could not come quickly enough for her. Thursday did of course arrive and Richard and Helen got up early to drive to London. They took Helen's little car and the journey was quick as they left at the crack of dawn, not a common occurrence for either of them in the past, but now they were base-altered, sleep was not required in quantity. They arrived at the flat at eight and made some coffee and breakfast. Richard watched breakfast TV and Helen read the paper they had picked up on the way to the flat from the newsagent at St. John's Wood station.

At nine a.m. the intercom to Richard's flat rang. Hans had caught the first flight out of Berlin to Heathrow and taken a taxi straight there. Richard, seeing Hans on the intercom screen, pressed the button to let him in telling him to use the lift and to come up to the penthouse. As he said that he pressed the button that allowed the lift up to that level. Helen and Richard were both there at the doors as it arrived at their floor. The doors opened and a tall, dark, strong-featured man with peppered greying hair stood there, wearing a beige trench coat. He stepped out and hugged Helen before stepping back and putting his hand out to Richard. He had a strong grip that did not surprise Richard, who returned the force evenly.

"Good-day," he said formally, "I am fascinate," which brought a smile to their faces.

"It's good to meet you at last," said Richard. "Come through."

"Take off that wet coat and I'll hang it up for you," Helen continued in German. Hans said, "Thank you, the rain has now stop in fact. I get wet at the airport." He looked at her in wonder at her newly revealed language skills. The two men moved through to the lounge where they settled down and Helen brought through cappuccinos for the three of them.

"Well," said Hans reverting to German, "I am truly intrigued as to what is so secret that we need to meet face to face in order to discuss it."

Helen spoke first. "Well Hans, what we want to discuss is not too far away from the research that you have been doing that no one believed in."

"However," Richard cut in quickly before she could say any more, "before we divulge this to you, we need you to sign this confidentiality agreement that I have drafted."

As he talked he reached over the back of the sofa to the table behind and picked up a single A4 sheet of paper. The words were in German. The Agreement bound Hans legally to keep what they were about to tell him secret and only to use it in conjunction with their joint research and development. Helen, slightly embarrassed by the need for this agreement, apologised to him but Hans, who by now was completely intrigued, signed willingly in order to find out more.

After taking a mouthful of coffee and pausing for a moment, Richard began to explain everything to Hans, allowing him to ask questions when he wanted. He did not want to mention his grandfather's file; he needed that to be his and Helen's secret. However, he quickly realised that Hans would need to know about it if they were to be believed, and in any case how else could he explain their base alteration without a second hypnotherapist who was a male. Why would they need him otherwise? No, he needed to know the full story. The explanation went much the same way as it did with Helen, some of the same questions arose and after an hour they got to the point where they would have to divulge Stuart's part in all of this. However Richard needed to know Helen's thoughts on Hans before doing so, it was imperative that they both fully trusted him. Excusing himself, Richard left the room, and went to the toilet. When he returned, he went straight to the kitchen to make more coffee and called Helen to assist him so that he had a chance to discuss how it was going.

Helen was absolutely fine with everything; she had always respected Hans, even though some of his ideas were considered to be a bit alternative, random even.

They returned to Hans with more coffee.

"Ah," Hans said, "this is good Cappuccino, no?"

"Yes," Richard replied, "it's an Arabic bean, very strong.

After a short pause while they all drank some coffee, he continued, "Hans, I want you to listen to a digital file. You will find this hard to believe, or given some of your ideas and research, maybe you won't. The file was made by my grandfather who died in January this year."

"Oh, I'm sorry," said Hans.

"Thank you," Richard said and he continued, "the ideas we have divulged to you today are in fact his and he told me about them in this digital file after his death. Be prepared to be surprised as the file is interactive."

Hans sat bolt upright and said "But how can that be?"

"Listen and you will learn," said Helen.

Hans looked rather disconcerted as Richard switched the system on and instructed it to play from where he last left off; perhaps he was questioning what he had let himself in for.

Immediately the file started to play.

"Hello Richard, Helen and Hans."

Hans looked curiously at the system. Who was this? Was he being set up, surely not, he knew Helen quite well and trusted her.

"Hans, I know you are questioning what is happening. You are probably wondering if this is for real," said Richard's grandfather as Hans was looking round the room for hidden cameras, thinking someone who was in another room was speaking to him and watching him.

"I can assure you it is real, the file is dynamic, capable of communication with the here and now."
Stuart continued to talk, telling Hans about how the file came about and eventually proving that it was really happening. "Hans, go to the window, look out and you will see a troupe of young school children in brown and yellow uniforms." Hans moved to the window to see just that. "But what does that prove?" he asked, "you could be looking out of other window of flat and seeing this. No?"
"Yes," came the response, "but in thirty seconds the third child in the line will trip and pull down the second child too," said Stuart's file. Hans watched intently, surely they could not set up such a stunt, he thought to himself?

As Hans watched, just as had been predicted, the third child fell pulling over the one in front of her. Hans turned back to the room, open-mouthed, but still sceptical. The voice continued, "Look out again." Hans looked out as directed. In twenty seconds there will be a clap of thunder, closely followed by a bolt of lightning, over in the park near by a lady dressed in a red coat. She will have her umbrella turned inside out by the force of the wind."
Sure enough exactly what Stuart predicted, happened.
"That's incredible," said Hans; realising that this last series of events could not have been set up. Richard did for Hans what he had done for Helen in explaining the entire journey to where they currently were and allowed Hans to hear excerpts of the played file as he fast-forwarded through it.

After he had time to recover and fully take in what was going on, Hans could not believe his luck. He and no other had been selected to share in such an amazing programme and to be party to information about the afterlife. He could now see why he was sworn to secrecy, although he did wonder how such an agreement could ever be enforced. Nevertheless, Hans was totally staggered by all of this, but completely on-board, so the likelihood of his breach of trust was minimal. After some further in-depth probing by Hans, he asked for some time on his own so he could think. Richard and Helen again retired to the kitchen.

Closing the door behind her she said, "What do you think?"

"I'm not sure, he seems sceptical."

"That's unusual; he's normally on the receiving end of scepticism. He's always pushing boundaries, I do hope he agrees."

"Going to be rather awkward if he doesn't, Helen," Richard stated throwing the palms of his hands up and out in front of him and back together in a wrenched self grip.

"Yes, yes it will be," she said as she knitted her eyebrows in a frown.

"Well, we will know soon," said Richard, "more Cappuccino?"

"Oh, yes please and I expect Hans will have another, he seems to like this blend."

Barely had the coffee been drawn when Hans knocked on the door to re-join them. Helen opened the door to see a smiling Hans, much more the demeanour she had come to know of him. He announced, "I have agreed and I am willing to take the part."

"I'm so pleased Hans, said Helen looking truly relieved.
"Me too," said Richard, "welcome on board old chap."
It was agreed that Hans too should be base altered sooner rather than later. He would carry out self-hypnosis as Helen had done then she would make the base alteration using DNA binary. However, they decided to wait until the weekend so that Hans had the opportunity to fully consider the implications of what he was about to become involved in, a cooling off period that was forced upon him, despite his protestations that he had indeed been won over.
"No, Hans. You need time to consider this on your own," Helen said finally and Hans realised she was bringing the discussion on the matter to a close for the moment. Almost in a daze, Hans took his leave of the pair to go to his London appointments. As he left, Helen and Richard reflected upon their own thoughts after preparing Hans and they discussed what they had thought when they had been in his position so they would be ready for his return that evening when undoubtedly he would have further questions for them.

Richard decided not to go in to work that day; rather he spent it with Helen. They needed a day off, so they spent the day strolling round London, visiting the National Art Gallery and the Natural History Museum. They had both been to these places on numerous occasions before, but this time their understanding of what they were looking at reached new levels. Their vastly improved intellect permitted them not only to see things that they had not noticed before, but also to analyse their findings in a completely different way. They discussed one particular point about the missing link in the Natural History Museum and were overheard by some teachers who were accompanying children on a school trip. Such was the depth of their understanding and complexity of their discussions, the teachers asked them to explain it to the children. Richard, who was never the best of communicators, looked at Helen. She smiled and obligingly gave the kids a clear and succinct view of how the missing link fitted into evolution. They thanked Helen for her mini lecture and the kids, who until then were extremely bored were now energised and were chattering away to each other about what they had just learnt. The teachers were greatly impressed and had never thought along these lines before. They asked Helen and Richard if they studied the subject and who they were, but Richard, keen to maintain anonymity dismissed them, saying it was merely a hobby. They said goodbye and moved on to the next exhibit, away from the school group.

"You were great with those kids," said Richard.

"I love kids; I used to be one you know," laughed Helen, as she skipped on down the corridor, clearly pleased with herself.

"No seriously," continued Richard, catching up with her, "you were very patient and clear. I could never have done that."

"I really do love kids, I want to have lots." Suddenly her mood changed, she looked despondent.

"What's the matter?" asked Richard.

"I've just remembered that we are going to have to limit everyone to only two children and I can't be any different, can I?" she asked with a questioning voice that almost requested a contrary answer from Richard, but it didn't come.

"No, no he said, I suppose not. But look on the bright side, you will be around long enough to enjoy not only grandchildren but great, great, great grandchildren."
As he said this he was realising the implications of a population explosion, something they had touched upon before but had not really discussed in detail. However, Helen was enthused by this idea. She smiled again and said "I hadn't thought of that, that's' wonderful."
At that Richard put to one side his thoughts of any population explosion; that was a subject for another time, he thought. They left the museum and walked the short distance to Harrods to have a late afternoon buffet at the Georgian Restaurant. Just as they were about to order Richard said, "Oh, what about Hans? He will need to eat when he gets back to the flat."
Helen replied, "No, he told me he was dining out with a colleague after his meeting; he didn't expect to be back until about eight."
Just then Helen's phone rang. It was Hans. He told her he was having considerable trouble concentrating on his meetings so he had excused himself from the later ones and had cancelled the dinner. He wanted to see them again to discuss more issues relating to SHINE. Helen asked Hans where he was and he said he was at Le Méridien Hotel in Piccadilly. She told him where they were and that this was quite close to his location. So he didn't get lost, they said they would travel to him and eat there too, killing two birds with one stone. Richard and Helen set off from Harrods to walk the relatively short distance to Piccadilly. When they got there Hans was sitting in the hotel café looking quite twitchy, wringing his napkin as he sat waiting for them.

"Oh, at last," Hans exclaimed as they walked up to him.
"Hi Hans, what's up?" said Helen picking up on his agitation.
"I am needing to ask you more question," he said, clearly worried and given away by his poor English.
"Fire away," said Richard, "I'm sure we will be able to answer anything you have to ask, after all we have been through the same as you."
"No," said Hans, "first we must eat. I am starve and have the shaking from no foods."
They took the lift to the first floor where there was a contemporary restaurant that overlooked Piccadilly. Having taken a seat near the full-height plate glass windows, they were given menus by a waitress and they wasted no time in choosing and ordering their meal. There was bread on the table and Hans tucked into that while they waited for their starter to arrive.
"So, Hans," said Helen, looking round to ensure no-one was close by who could hear them, "what's troubling you?"
"I have been doing the thinking and it is the base-alteration, I am concern about," he replied. "Not method, the altered being. Part of the fun of being is the learning and I don't suddenly want to be a genius knows all it."
"Know it all," interjected Richard changing to German, partly because his German was infinitely better than Hans' English and partly to minimise the potential for being overheard and understood by other diners.
"And you won't be Hans. We have been base-altered and we still have much to learn. The change does not give immediate knowledge, in fact the opposite, you will have a new and amazing capacity for learning, much

more than you ever thought possible before. Your brain will be a damp sponge waiting to be soaked with knowledge. Your lifetime will be much longer and you will have the ability to learn throughout that period. To give you an example, only today we went to a museum and were able to look at something that we have looked at many times before, but today we understood it in an entirely different way, to reach a new and I believe correct conclusion relating to evolution."

"Yes," interjected Helen, "it was indeed amazing, so you see there really is no need to worry Hans, you will continue to learn but in a far more satisfying and effective way."

Hans sat back in his chair and dropped his tense look. He seemed reassured and at ease with the answer he had been given.

"So, you are still you inside, despite the base alteration, still individuals" he said more as a statement than a question.

"Yes, absolutely," Richard and Helen said together. Richard and Helen laughed and Hans followed suit slightly behind them, after all he wasn't as quick minded, yet. Over dinner they continued to discuss SHINE in German. By the end of the meal, Hans said he was entirely comfortable with the prospect and more importantly, his involvement. The three of them took a taxi back to Richard's flat and, after a nightcap, Hans asked to be excused as he was exhausted from the day's discussions and he retired to bed. Helen and Richard bade him goodnight. They by contrast were not yet tired, and they would retire later so that they could wake at the same time as Hans.

16

The next day was to have been a day off for Hans after his day of meetings so he could go sightseeing. When he excused himself from the meetings the day before, he had tentatively rearranged them again for the Friday, knowing he would be busy on the Saturday with SHINE and his plans were then to return to Berlin on the Sunday. He telephoned his colleagues who confirmed they could still see him and that put paid to any personal time for him. He set off and said he would see Richard and Helen that evening for dinner at a local restaurant, his treat to repay them for their hospitality.

After breakfast and when Hans had left, Richard and Helen decided to review the programme for SHINE, now that all the key players were in place. Richard was also eager to re-visit the population issue. After a brief and conclusive discussion about population, they agreed that the way forward was the publication of a paper in *The Lancet*. Recognising that they would get much flak from this, with their vastly superior brainpower, they carefully worded their entry to avoid any questions that could not be answered without the need to expose Sir Stuart and thus the after-life. At this stage they also did not want to alert people to the increased life span that they knew was also available. The only other difficult area they saw was DNA binary. They could hear the questions now. Where had it come from? How did they learn it? The explanation they decided upon was to say that it came from sub-hypnosis of Richard after experimentation by Helen and Hans, where Helen carried out the second level of hypnosis under Hans' guidance. They said the language was found deep in Richard's subconscious and that, at the time, they did not realise the implications of the language. They would continue to explain that they then discovered base-alteration accidentally by applying the language at sub-hypnosis level. After all, they reasoned, many medical findings are fortunate accidents, so why not this one? The entry was couched under the heading of 'Increased Brain Power Through Sub-Hypnosis'. They decided to say that Helen Harrison wrote the paper jointly with Hans Groeber. Innocuous enough they thought, subject to Hans' agreement.

On the Saturday, Hans' base-alteration went without a hitch with Hans placing himself into self-hypnosis and Helen carrying out the second part at sub-hypnosis level using the DNA binary. Similar to their own reactions, Hans went into overdrive initially and then crashed out after exhausting his energy reserves with the new level of brainpower. When he came round from his sleep an hour or so later, he had many new questions and the three of them spent the next few hours discussing the way forward. They showed Hans the proposed publication and he quickly agreed that it was a good way to progress matters. Hans left them as agreed on the Sunday to return to Berlin and Helen and Richard returned to Cambridge after dropping Hans off at the airport on the way. He had managed to change his flight to one which departed from Stansted, which was much more convenient than Heathrow. They all agreed to push forward with SHINE and clearly, the most pressing issue was funding, so they sent in their paper and it was published in the May edition of *The Lancet.* It was published as they had agreed as, 'Increased Brain Power Through Sub-Hypnosis by Helen Harrison and Hans Groeber' and it was received with the usual scepticism attached to papers on hypnotherapy and hypnosis. However, at the same time as *The Lancet* published, SHINE issued a press release to The Times and letters to MP's advising them of their findings. One MP, Michael Williams, who was also a doctor, picked up on the proposal from the three sources and requested a meeting with the directors of SHINE. They prepared themselves thoroughly for the meeting, running through every possible question that could be raised and discussing answers that would overcome any possible objections that could be raised. This was of course a relatively easy task with their superior intellect, but neither of them was entirely comfortable manipulating people, even though it was absolutely necessary in this case to maintain Sir Stuart's anonymity. It simply had to be done, so like the committed individuals they were, they just got on with the job at hand.

They met Michael Williams on Saturday 12th May at his home in Harley Street. They travelled down from Cambridge in the morning, arriving at the appointed

time at a heavy oak door to an almost gothic style red brick building. An extremely attractive, dark haired, smartly dressed young lady opened the door after a few moments and invited them in when they divulged their identity. They were ushered into the library and told that Mr Williams would be with them in a few minutes. They knew from doing their homework that he was the MP for Westminster, which included St John's Wood, so Richard's flat was in his constituency. This, thought Richard, was indeed fortuitous as, if he was interested, Michael would be seen to be promoting the interests of one of his constituents, which could not be misconstrued as the MP being self-indulgent and would remove the need for him to then consult another MP for local support. The door opened and an elderly gentleman of around sixty-five years walked in. He had a slightly portly figure and a cheery smile, ruddy complexion and receding grey hair. He looked quite distinguished in his mustard-coloured waistcoat and green tweed suit, every bit a doctor. Helen immediately took a liking to the man. She thought he looked trustworthy and she squeezed Richard's hand under the table to signify this, but Richard mistook the gesture for nerves, which indeed he was feeling. Pleasantries were exchanged between the three and Michael offered them both teas, which they accepted. Michael rang the bell next to the fireplace. The young lady that had let them in returned and Michael requested, "Tea for three please and some of those nice biscuits you gave me yesterday, thank you Emily."
Emily said, "Yes Sir," and she slipped out of the room quietly closing the door behind her.

The small talk continued for a while with Michael and Richard exchanging thoughts on the virtues of living in Westminster. Helen added that she loved the architecture and commented on how beautiful the doctor's house was.

"Do you practice from here too?" she asked.

"I used to," Michael responded, "before I became an MP. Now I just live here during the week. At the weekend, I return to my wife, we live on the coast at Eastbourne; she loves it there. It's an exception for me to be here on a Saturday."

"Well," said Richard, "thank you for seeing us at the weekend; it's very good of you."

"Oh it's no problem," said Michael, "in fact my wife is coming up to London today, and we are going to a show tonight."

At that the door opened and Emily came in with the tea. She placed the tray on the coffee table and asked, "Will that be all, Sir?"

"Yes thank you Emily," he said turning to his guests and immediately back to Emily. "Oh just one thing more, Emily; I will be here for another hour or so with my guests. If you would be so kind as to clear up when we have gone, you may leave after that and my wife and I will see you in the morning."

"Very good Sir, thank you Sir," she said as she left the room.

"She's a good girl," said Michael. "There are not so many around these days who are willing to be in a serving role and be pleased about it."

"No, I suppose not," said Helen, not really knowing what he meant, as she had never had servants but in

her head thinking that perhaps it was like having a willing waitress in a restaurant.
"In fact," Michael continued, "that's one of my questions relating to your paper in *The Lancet*. I must admit, I am very intrigued, but at the same time..."
"Sceptical?" suggested Richard.
"No, no, my dear boy; not sceptical, cautious. Amongst other things, I'm worried about people like Emily in your new world order, how will she fit in?"

Richard and Helen had already decided to run through the concept of base-alteration in more detail for the MP before the case for setting up SHINE centres was put forward and now seemed to be the perfect time to do that in response to his question. They explained that after base-alteration, there would still be a difference in levels of IQ and that in some sense the current hierarchy would remain. For the time being however, although it would have served their argument better, they did not let on about the increased lifespan and that there would be plenty of time for people to sample many different careers and jobs throughout their extended lives. As a doctor Michael's other main concern was the physical and mental effect on anyone who was base altered. Helen told Michael she too had been concerned about that, but she said it had made no change to her or to Richard and Hans, all of whom had been base-altered. Michael, until that moment, was unaware that they had been in his words 'processed' and was utterly amazed at how apparently unaffected they were by the change. However, he realised that human tests would be impossible but that the three who had undergone the process could be considered as tested if they maintained their 'normality' and he said that further monitoring of their mental status would be essential. To appease his concern, Richard and Helen agreed to ongoing monitoring of their health, but of course they knew from what Sir Stuart had already told them that there were no adverse affects of the IQ improvement or indeed the lifespan enhancement.

Richard laid out his long-term plans for the SHINE centres, including his own funding abilities, and Michael was impressed by his personal commitment. That made Richard feel dreadful as he knew the funds would be from the investments he was able to make from the insider information given to him by Sir Stuart, but that was unavoidable now, he was committed. Nevertheless, he was trying to come to terms with the means of funding foisted upon him by his grandfather and the more he thought about it and the more he heard of the so called 'Fat Cat' payouts, the less this bothered him. Every day, during the recent world recession there were more and more reports of obscene bonuses being paid out to supposed top financiers, Richard reflected. If they were so clever, how come they didn't have a clue what was going on with all this sub-prime mortgage lending? 'Sub-prime', he reflected evaluating the term as he thought it, suddenly coming to the realisation that he had the power to eradicate sub-prime by sub-hypnosis and base-alteration, a fitting end to the expression, he thought. He also took solace in the fact that, initially at least; much of the investment was from the inheritance from his grandfather's will.

As Richard drifted back to the room from his personal thoughts, he became aware that Helen, who knew only too well his reticence to pursue the investment funding route, was asking Michael about alternative or additional funding, government funding. Michael was agreeing to look into the possibility of government funding for the centres to augment what Richard was prepared to commit. Richard and Helen thanked Michael for his time and interest and said they looked forward to hearing from him. So that he could become completely au fait with the process of base-alteration and their proposals for SHINE they left him a dossier that Michael placed on his desk. Richard emphasised the need for secrecy and asked Michael to be very careful who he permitted to see the documentation.

Michael concluded the meeting by saying he would be back to them by the end of the month. As they parted, Helen wished Michael a good evening at the show with his wife, asking, "What are you seeing?" Michael replied "Oh, we're going to see the new show by Lloyd Webber, I forget its actual name."
Richard said, "Oh, you mean *Love Never Dies*. I've heard from my parents that it's a great show, do enjoy it."
"That's the one, thank you, we will. Goodbye Richard, goodbye Helen."
"Goodbye Michael." They said together.

The summer sun was beaming down as they walked away from the door in Harley Street towards Euston Road, through Regents Park and back to Richard's flat at St John's Wood where they had parked. As they ambled along, they reflected on the meeting and were extremely pleased with the outcome; it seemed to them that they were at last making progress. Richard told Helen of the thoughts he had during the meeting regarding the sub-prime issue. Helen retorted that she had wondered where he was for a few moments as she had noted he had drifted off somewhere, telling him also that she didn't think that Michael had noticed, fortunately. There was little they could do until they heard back from Michael so without even entering the flat they collected the car and returned to Cambridge. They would telephone Hans on the way to update him on the outcome of the meeting.

The rest of the month was taken up by work for them both and Hans too was busy in Berlin. Helen spent some time with her parents as they were beginning to think she had moved out, which she had pretty much as she now saw Richard on almost a daily basis. She continued her hypnotherapy consulting and was tempted to delve further than she had in the past, but knew she should not, so resisted the pull, although she was now gaining a greater understanding of her subject and re-read books on the subject in her spare time. Meanwhile, Richard was making rapid personal progress on his latest research project, but he could not divulge the full extent of that to any of his colleagues yet. Hans was busy rewriting his theories following his base-alteration, but similarly he too could not discuss them with anyone. To keep themselves from going stir crazy, all three kept in close touch with each other, particularly of course Richard and Helen, to discuss their personal achievements and their frustrations. Richard was now heavily into fitness training and Helen assisted to keep focused on that, as the Olympics were looming at the end of July.

By the time Michael Williams got back to Richard, it was Monday 26th June. It was good news. Although it had taken some time, Michael had not been idle. He had mustered the support of some of the Government's most influential MPs and had even spoken about it to the Prime Minister and had obtained his support to take it to the next stage, the set up of SHINE to research the proposals further. A Bill for the funding was to be put before Parliament prior to the summer recess. It was being drafted as they spoke and Richard, Helen and Hans were to attend a briefing on Wednesday at the House of Commons to clarify some final matters. They thanked Michael for his efforts to which he responded that they were very welcome. After all, this could be a feather in his cap too as champion of this initiative. Richard telephoned Hans immediately to give him the good news. Hans' mobile rang; he answered "Guten tag, Hans Groeber."
"Hans, it's me, Richard."
"Ah, Richard, what newses?
"You need to be here by Wednesday, we have a meeting at the House of Commons at eleven a.m. can you make it?" he said resisting the temptation to correct Hans' English.
"Are you kiddings?" he replied, "I'll be there tomorrow night."
"You can stay with me Hans," Richard replied, "but it's probably easier if you make your own way to my flat, you know the way now don't you?"
"Ja, Yes, see you at about eight p.m. okay?"

"Yes, that's fine, see you then, bye."
Richard removed the phone from his ear and stroked it to end the call. He looked up at Helen, who had been listening.
"He does make me laugh you know with his English usage."
"I know," she replied, "but his heart is in the right place. What I can't understand is why with his enhanced IQ he doesn't correct himself. Habit I suppose," she continued, answering her own question.
"Possibly, but it's quite endearing, I hope he doesn't change, something would be missing if everyone in the future could speak perfectly in any language they chose Where would the fun be in that?" Richard responded.
"Zo, ve vill zee heem tomorrow zen," Richard mimicked, over-egging it.
"Ya, aber you are zo cruel," Helen barely managed to say as she was laughing so much. Richard too had tears of joy running down his cheeks as he laughed at their playful mickey-taking. As they finally regained control they hugged each other in the realisation that their dream was beginning to happen.

Helen and Richard travelled to London by train on Tuesday afternoon. It was a leisurely journey in first class, both preferring that level of travel so they could work, but they never did. They talked and watched the countryside go by as they had lunch. Hans arrived that night exactly when he had planned, he was so precise, and they spent the night eating a Chinese meal delivered from a local restaurant and discussing the upcoming meeting at the House of Commons. They retired at three a.m. which was early for them but quite soon enough for them to be fresh for the MP's questions. In the event, the morning was beautiful and sunny and the sun streaming through the gap in the curtains in Richard's bedroom woke Helen at about 7:00 a.m. She got up, donned a dressing gown and went to the kitchen to prepare some coffee and breakfast. Hans was next to rise and he came to the kitchen saying, "Guten morgen, I could smell ze coffee, it's always zo great here, Italian, ja?"

"Morning, yes it is today," Helen responded, "and some croissants with English jam, a bit of a cultural mishmash really."

"Ja and a German eating it, no?" Hans laughed at his own attempt at a joke.

"What's funny?" asked Richard as he walked into the room.

"Oh, you had to be there," said Helen, raising her eyebrows to Richard out of sight of Hans.

"Ah, cappuccino," Richard said, changing the subject, "just the ticket."

They all settled down to breakfast. After breakfast Hans went off to finish dressing.

"We'll leave at ten, Hans," Richard shouted as Hans walked towards the bedroom he had been given.

"Okay," he replied.

Helen and Richard also went to their bedroom to dress for the meeting.

"A suit I think. Which one, Helen?"

Helen smiled and moved to his wardrobe to select some clothes for him. He picked out a shirt, which she put back, raising her eyebrows as she did so and picking another and, before he could choose, a tie that matched the shirt.

"Thanks, I don't know what I'd do without you," he said.
"I know." she replied, smiling.

Soon they were all ready and it was only nine o'clock so they sat down to watch the BBC News channel for a while before they left the flat at ten as they had agreed. The Olympics were looming and the news was full of it. Yet again the question of one of the athlete's gender arose, this time before any records had been set.
"At least yours won't be questioned. Richard."
"Helen!" Richard exclaimed, embarrassed in front of Hans who just laughed, but the news item caused the three to discuss the subject and they thought that perhaps this was something that they could change in the future by genetic alteration under sub-hypnosis. They agreed that they could most likely save a lot of heartache for men and women who were trapped in the wrong body. Other news items provoked equally relevant discussion amongst them so the hour passed very quickly and soon it was time to leave the flat.
Downstairs, Richard hailed a black cab; they were plentiful at that time, with many drivers at the beginning of their shift heading into town and taking a short cut through Regents Park. A cab stopped, they all got in and Richard said, "House of Commons please driver."
"You got it Governor," the cabby replied as he set off in a southerly direction through the London traffic, which was relatively light. Hans commented upon the ability to move around in London without too many traffic jams.

"Yes," replied Richard, "The Congestion Zone charges have helped London to move a bit faster than it used to."
"Can you open a window please, Richard? It's getting very warm in here," Helen asked.
As Richard was about to move to open a window, from the speaker system in the cab came: "You're awright darlin'; I got air conditionin'. See the button on the roight 'and door, yeah, press that and it'll cool you darn."
Somewhat surprised by the interjection, Helen leant across Richard and pressed the cool button on the panels. Immediately, a cold stream of air blasted forcefully into the passenger area. Helen looked back at the controls and pushed the fan button to reduce the force.
"Sound, there you go." said the cabbie smiling in the rear view mirror.
"Thank you," she said somewhat irritated that he had been listening to their conversation. Thank goodness they had not been discussing SHINE, she thought as she pressed a third button that was labelled 'Mute'.
"Can you hear me now, driver?" she asked. There was no response.
"Good, but we had better not discuss anything important here I think. You never know, do you?" she said, more as a statement than a question. Hans just smiled; he had no idea what the cab driver had just said.
They spent the rest of the journey giving Hans a sightseeing tour of the buildings they passed in the cab, without the interruption of the cabbie. That was perhaps a shame, thought Richard, as these cabbies were often a mine of information and perhaps in his

own way, he could have added to the information that Richard and Helen imparted to Hans, after all neither of them were native Londoners. Native or not, they knew when they were approaching Westminster and sat forward on their seats in preparation for their arrival.
"Here we are Hans," said Richard as the cab stopped, blocking the single lane of traffic. Richard, noticing this, was quick to pay the cabbie including a tip. Causing a delay didn't seem to bother the driver at all despite the fact he was being hooted by impatient drivers behind him. In fact when he took off he spun round in a U-turn further irritating the following traffic, shouting a "Thank you, Governor," to Richard as he did so.

Michael Williams met Richard, Helen and Hans at the door to the House of Commons. He briefed them as to the protocol of the meeting, which was to be held in one of the annexes. After signing them in through Security, and following a search of Helen's handbag, Hans's attaché case and Richard's bulging inside jacket pocket, spotted by an alert security guard, they were allowed into the Public Area of the House. From there the four of them entered a side room where there were already four other people, two ladies and two gentlemen. Michael made the introductions. The first lady was the Home Secretary and Minister for Women and Equality and of course the Prime Minister needed no introduction, nor did his Deputy. High praise indeed, thought Richard. They are taking this very seriously with such top calibre officials to meet us. The second lady was Sally Green; she was there to take notes on the meeting and was Michael's secretary. Sally asked if anyone would like tea or coffee, which, when that was affirmed, she poured and handed round.

The PM thanked them all for coming and explained that the reason for the meeting was so the parliamentarians could fully understand SHINE and base-alteration and how it would affect the country, indeed the world. He said the dossier prepared by Richard and Helen, and lent by them to Michael, had been a very informative and frank synopsis, but there remained a few areas that needed to be discussed and some ground rules that needed to be set. Richard had feared exactly that; ground rules set by Government! Rules set by Government and there for the breaking by the Government he thought to himself. Not good, but he went with the programme for the moment. The PM continued asking each of the three visitors to give a brief synopsis of themselves prior to questions being asked, which they did, explaining their individual backgrounds. Each of them then detailed the process of base-alteration and how it had affected them personally and although the Ministers realised that their visitors' minds were superior to their own, that did not at all intimidate the MP's; although before the meeting they had feared they might be. This went a long way to reassuring them that base-alteration was indeed a good thing. In fact many of the questions they had prepared simply fell by the wayside, answered by the three's addresses. There were others though, so when Hans, who spoke last, had finished speaking, the Home Secretary started off the question process.

Without exception all of the Ministers' questions were reservations that the three of them had already dealt with before their base-alteration and so they were able to respond and appease with ease. Helen, Richard and Hans had prepared very well; in fact they were aware of many questions that the Ministers had not thought to ask that they nonetheless had answers to and Richard was in no doubt that was because he and the other two were base-altered. They did not feel the need to divulge more information than was requested. Richard's reckoning was that if the three of them had come up with more testing questions and were happy with their own answers, so should the Ministers be. In any case, their superior level questions may just serve to confuse and so better to keep quiet. Additionally of course, they had the knowledge from his grandfather that everything would work out. As the probing ceased, the PM continued saying he recognised that this knowledge was now available and that it, the base alteration, would happen in any event, either with or without them, but he believed the correct way to go about this was to embrace the advances and to go with it. However, he stressed that the Government needed to be fully conversant with what it all meant, as the House would be in uproar when the debate took place and he and the Home Secretary needed to have all the answers. Also, they would make no bones about it; they wanted their party to be first to benefit from the advances, the first to be base-altered.

Richard shuffled in his seat and was about to interject when Helen kicked him under the table and wrote 'wait' on her pad.

"Also," said the Deputy Prime Minister, speaking for the first time, "we need to be in the forefront of this, in the driving seat so to speak. There is no getting away from it; this can do Britain no harm at all. We're all too aware that we have been losing favour with the rest of the world recently, but this could be our turning point, our Waterloo."
He carried on becoming quite animated, holding his lapel and thrusting his chest forward, he almost stood up. Clearly this man had ideas of even greater power, thought Richard, which brought him back to think of the 'ground rules' and the, 'our Government first' statement earlier. Richard could also see that Hans, being German, was not best pleased by that little outburst and Helen had given him the same sign as she had given Richard earlier as she had noticed too. Finally, the PM sat back, looked at the three of them in turn and at Michael and said, "Before I conclude this meeting, do you have any questions for us?"
Michael, who had remained quiet throughout the meeting, but had been observing, stood up and said, "I think we would all benefit from a ten minute comfort break and I am sure our guests would like to confer before concluding the meeting."
They all nodded and the PM agreed that they should meet back in the room in ten minutes at twelve-thirty. They all left the room except Sally who stayed to replenish their cups.

Once outside and the three were alone, Richard said to Hans, "I can see that was not to your taste Hans."

"Damn right it's not." he retorted, "However, I em now too intelligent to start war on it, but this is joint effort by Britain und Germany."
"Hardly old chap, it's international, we just happen to be British and you German. I do see your point, although strictly speaking it's my idea so it is English. We'll make sure that recognition is given where recognition is due."
Helen cut in, "Yes and don't forget *The Lancet* publication. That predates the Bill, the timeline will speak for itself."
Richard continued, "This chap is just getting a bit above his station, he will realise that when he is base-altered Hans, don't worry."
"Vell, okay, if you are sure," Hans replied, looking like a schoolboy who had just had a telling off.
"More worrying I thought is this idea of us creating a super-race whereby we base-alter the governing party first. Can you imagine?" he laughed. "We do that then they rescind the Bill. Not a chance. We will have to get that one clear right now."
"Or what," said Helen, "there's no deal? No, we need to come up with something that prevents that from happening, something we have not divulged yet, something that makes the base-alteration order random thus no party or indeed other faction can gain an edge."
"I agree, but we've got five minutes chaps," Richard reminded them. "Okay, thinking cap on Helen, you too Hans."
They sat down on the seats in the corridor outside the room they had been using and concentrated their thoughts for a few moments. Suddenly, Richard

jumped up and said, "I have it, I have the answer to randomness; it's radicalisation."
"Go on," said Helen intrigued. Well, as you both know there is a process of learning that goes on after the base-alteration. We are still experiencing it and indeed I believe we will forever continue to learn just as we did before base-alteration."
"Ja okay," said Hans, "but how does zis assist us now?"
"Well...," Richard was about to explain then decided not to, "no, anyone got any other ideas?"
"No," they said together.
"Then we have to go with my idea, you will see what it is when we're back in the room."

Just then the huge oak door opened and Sally popped her head round and asked if they were coming back in. Richard led the way and they took their original seats. The others were seconds behind them and the meeting resumed exactly on time.
"So," said the PM, "punctuality, that's what I like to see. Now, we need to know if you have any issues you would like to ask us"
"Yes," said Richard, "you mentioned ground rules. What are they please?"
"Actually," said the PM, "we can't answer that yet, but there are bound to be some stipulations that Ministers will want to impose that come from the House debate, so can you bear with us on that and we will report back to you? Nothing will be a deal breaker on this, we cannot allow it."
'No, a problem isn't a problem until it's there', Richard thought, 'and when it's there it's a problem and possibly a deal breaker'. However, in this case he was

right, there could be no deal breakers; it had to happen. Richard then realised he could use the Minister's own words, that were being recorded verbatim by Sally, to tie him down, so he came back with, "No, nothing can be a deal breaker on this one, Sir." Richard was suddenly making the matter very formal, "And that brings me to your request that your party be first to be base altered; that cannot happen."

"And why not?" questioned the PM, sitting bolt upright at this statement.

"It's a matter of radicalisation, Sir."

"What on earth has that to do with this, Mr Harper?"

The PM was now looking rather hot under the collar. He did not like this at all; but by the same token realised that he had just agreed to nothing being a deal breaker. Helen and Hans were also sitting forward now, as they too were very interested in this as they had no idea what Richard was about to say.

Richard continued, amused by the fact that he now felt he had the PM in a headlock that Jackie Pallow would have been proud of. He had never been a fan of governments, considering them a necessary evil, no matter which party was in power. They had all, in the past, cut his department's research budgets from time to time which irked him greatly.

"Well Sir, as I am sure you know radicalisation is the exact opposite of conservativism."

"Yes, yes." The PM agreed, shaking his head in a way that indicated get on with it man, get to the point.

Richard paused deliberately; he was going to enjoy this moment. A little white lie but absolutely necessary, given the gravity of the life-changing programme they were about to embark upon.

"Sir, in the very early days after base-alteration, there is a period of intense learning as the brain creates many new neural pathways and takes up all the slack, ties up all the loose ends if you like, of the brain as it was before the base-alteration." Well at least that bit is true he thought. "This leaves the brain in a very susceptible condition where it is open to coercion from others. If we were to alter all of your party at the same time, there is a strong possibility that you would contaminate each other with your similar thoughts to a point where radicalisation might take place. It might not be as overt as Taliban radicalisation, I doubt if any of you would become suicide bombers, but in its own way could be equally as damning to humanity. In effect, you would no longer be conservatives, and we don't want that do we, Sir?"
Richard smiled a false conciliatory smile. Helen and Hans smiled too but theirs was rather more like one of relief as they had not known what Richard was going to say. Brilliant, thought Helen, absolutely brilliant, but then he was.

The Home Secretary, who had left most of the discussion to the PM, was nodding in agreement but the DPM was looking rather shell shocked, his master plan for his Party's supremacy had disappeared as quickly and surely as Ministers leaving the House for the summer recess. He felt that even as PM designate, he could not argue with Richard's ground rules. It seemed the tables had been turned; it was now Richard's game. The Government wanted what the three of them could offer, as they could see the power it would give them; however, they would have to accept everyone moving

up the IQ scales together. Richard was pleased. He reckoned that if this went ahead and that was now extremely likely, the status quo would at worst be maintained, but most likely with greater intelligence and understanding the world should be a better place.
"Oh, one final thing," Richard said. "I will personally be the principal funder in the SHINE centres so they will not be government run, although you will have a say in financial and moral issues."
Richard said this almost as a passing shot in a very take it or leave it manner, but he knew he had the PM on the run and he was going to make the most of it. This was his ground rule and he needed to stick to it, so he was to be the majority shareholder and maintained the final say, as his grandfather had advised him. When he had recovered his composure, the PM advised them that, as the issue was so important, the Bill was to be read on 19th July a few days before the summer recess. It would be heard in the House of Lords the day after.
"Three weeks from now," said Richard. "That's good; we will look forward to the outcome," he said, thinking what brilliant timing. The Ministers would either not be there, having left early for the summer or, those that were in attendance, would be in good humour in expectation of the break. The party of three thanked the Ministers for their time and they took their leave, Richard picking up his dossier as he departed the room. They also thanked Michael who was staying on at the House. Sally, no doubt pleased to have stopped the typing she had been doing furiously during the entire meeting, showed them to the exit. As they reached the vast door she said, "I will send you a copy of my

meeting minutes by secure email later today Mr Harper, after the DPM's approval. Goodbye."
"Thank you Sally," Richard replied as the others said goodbye.

Outside, the sun was bright and so was the mood of the three of them, very pleased with the way the meeting had gone.
"Richard," said Helen coyly, "you were playing with him; that's very naughty."
"Ja, it was very funny, no?" said Hans. They all laughed as they headed towards town for some well-deserved lunch. A successful day they all thought as they strolled cheerfully through Trafalgar Square and up St. Martin's Lane towards their intended lunch destination in the relative seclusion at the Brasserie Max at the Covent Garden Hotel. After lunch, they parted company at Leicester Square station to catch the Piccadilly Line where Hans headed westbound towards Heathrow airport and Helen and Richard went eastbound to Kings Cross to catch a late afternoon train back to Cambridge.

17

Richard and Helen had travelled down to St. John's Wood to be near Westminster in case they were needed for any reason, it just felt right that they should be on hand. They had taken the day off, but wished they hadn't as the day had dragged terribly. In the event they were not needed and now they were waiting around for a phone call about the result of the Bill's reading. Finally the telephone in Richard's flat rang at four p.m. It was the call they had been waiting for, but when it came they both looked at the device that was ringing on the lounge coffee table as though it were an alien thing. What would the answer be? The scale of the base-alteration programme hung on this call. They looked at each other willing the other to answer the call. Neither did, it stopped ringing.

"No," cried Richard, "why didn't you answer it?"

"I thought you would," said Helen, "it's your flat."

They had both been on edge all day, but that hurt Richard. By now he considered it to be her home too.

"That's not fair," he retorted.

"No, you're right, I'm sorry, it's just that this will change the rest of our lives and ..."

The phone rang again and they both rushed to answer it. Helen won, being closer to it than Richard.
"Hello, Helen Harrison."
Richard, who had stopped in his tracks when Helen reached the phone first, lost all thought of what the call was about. All he heard was her words 'Helen Harrison. This was the first time he had realised how he could not be without her, he wanted her close at all times, forever. He wanted her to be answering that telephone 'Hello, Helen Harper'. He was looking at her so intently and with so much longing that she stopped talking, said excuse me to the person on the other end of the phone and said to Richard "Are you okay, you've suddenly gone very pale?"
"Yes, yes I'm fine." He raised a smile and came back to earth, but he thought that was very sweet, she had stopped in mid-call, a call of monumental importance to check on how he was. This beautiful lady was definitely the woman for him.
Helen returned to the call. "Sorry, Michael, what were you saying?" She listened for a few moments and then said, "Thank-you for all your efforts, no doubt we will be speaking soon. Have a good holiday. Goodbye."
She turned to Richard with a deadpan face and looked at him.
"I don't care if it's bad news," he said, "just tell me."
He thought her unsmiling face said it all, but he really didn't care at that point because he had just made up his mind to get married. Now all he needed to know was whether she wanted to too. All at once she beamed and flung her arms out to him, hugging and kissing him and trying to talk at the same time.

"Yes, mwah, it's a yes, mwah, they've agreed to, mwah, funding, mwah, and to the, mwah, British SHINE centres, mwah."

Richard could not believe it, there had apparently been a fierce debate, but no one tried to scupper the Bill and the House of Commons had agreed to everything they had hoped for and more. Helen also told him that it had been a close call on the Government funding for SHINE though, as Ministers were still reeling over the true cost of hosting the Olympic Games. Just the Lords' decision tomorrow now he thought, but that should be a formality. Still holding her, he pushed her to arms length so he could look at her. They were both beaming now and Helen said, "I love you, Richard, I will remember this day forever."
Richard, immediately responded "I love you too." and as he said it he continued to hold her, gazing wistfully into her eyes. He was thinking that only a few minutes earlier he had decided to marry this beautiful, intelligent, caring and funny woman. He thought back in time to his younger days when he imagined how he might ask a woman to marry him. Take her to an unusual place, the top of a mountain for instance, or a far distant location, or a place that was special for them both and then pop the question. Pop the question, he had used that term in his youth, but he hated that now. It seemed so inappropriate, like you were sneaking it in between other questions so the recipient wouldn't realise. No, he would not pop the question; he would be forthright and ask it now, it seemed so fitting. She had just said she would never forget this day, why not make it a day to remember for more than one reason?

The beginning of SHINE and the day he asked Helen Harrison to become Helen Harper. This thought process, despite his improved IQ, had taken a little while and Helen was now looking at him rather curiously. A furrow developed in her brow as she said, "What's up Richard, you look perplexed, is this not what you wanted?"

Richard looked at her as he had done when she was on the phone; in complete awe.

"H-Helen." he stammered, something that did not happen very often these days. He paused to gain some composure. "Will you marr ....".

Before he had finished, she pulled him towards her and said, "Yes, Richard, yes I will marry you."

He was so shocked; he hadn't even had time to get down on one knee.

"Yes?"

"Yes," she said again planting a kiss firmly on his lips. They hugged closely for a few minutes, both deep in their thoughts of what they had just agreed to. They were interrupted by the phone ringing again. Fearful that Michael had forgotten to tell them something, they broke their embrace and Richard answered the call. It was Hans; he had been patiently waiting in Berlin for a call from them. In their passion, they had forgotten all about him.

"Hi Hans, yes sorry we have been tied up on something. It's fantastic news Hans our government has agreed to all we wanted. SHINE is now on the first rung of the ladder. Hans asked Richard what that meant.

"Sorry, I mean the first stage has been reached," he said, changing to an expression Han's would understand. Hans would not forget that now though,

their new brains were soaking everything up, like the young and eager brain of a child.
Helen gestured to take the phone from Richard.
"Hans, Helen wants to speak with you. I'll speak to you later in the week. Bye."
Richard handed the phone to Helen.
"Hans, I have some more wonderful news. Richard has just asked me to marry him and I have agreed, I am going to be Mrs Helen Harper."
She giggled as she told him, the first of many to hear their news.
"Thank-you Hans, I will tell him. Bye."
She put the phone down.
"He says you're a lucky man."
"Don't I know it."

Helen knew she should have told her parents first, but Hans was in Berlin so there was time for that. She mentioned that to Richard and he suddenly realised he hadn't asked Helen's father for her hand. Cardinal sin, he thought. Worried about this error he and Helen discussed what to do and agreed to go to Cambridge that weekend to ask her father's permission. The ring would have to wait until after then. Damn, thought Richard, an IQ of 292 and still I get it wrong, but Helen seemed ecstatically happy and said she would be marrying him no matter what her father said so maybe it didn't matter. With personal matters agreed, they decided they should work on SHINE for an hour or so to set the agenda for the future. They decided to consult the oracle, Richard's grandfather, so Richard ordered the multimedia system to switch on and play the special file.

"Hello you two," Stuart said sounding decidedly upbeat. "Congratulations."
They both laughed, "So now two people know," said Helen."
"No, one person knew months ago, me," came the response from Richard's grandfather. "You two were destined for each other; it was only a matter of time."
"Of course, you knew, but we never thought to ask when it would be," said Helen.
"I would not have told you in any event, some things are better as surprises," Stuart replied.
Helen was burning to ask whether she would have children, but thought that might be inappropriate so early in their engagement and also she had sensed that Stuart's reply relating to personal information was as much a warning for them not to ask such questions. Stuart continued, "Everything is going to plan with SHINE; it's now time for you to start investing more aggressively, you will need serious amounts of money soon." Richard had never thought of doing anything aggressively except in sport, but took the advice of his grandfather making notes on the advice he was giving for his action the next day.

"Grandad, something has been bothering me." "Yes," his grandfather replied, "I know. It's how much of the file is left and when should it be played?"
"Yes." Richard replied, never quite getting used to his grandfather's insight.
"Well, Richard, the file has another ten minutes of play until the end. After that you are on your own. Well, you and Helen and your children and friends and..."

"Children, you said children, so I, I mean we, will have two, the new limit!" she exclaimed.
"Yes, I can tell you that much, but I won't say what they will be, or when it will happen, only that they will be healthy. If you like, you can call one Stuart."
"A boy!" Helen interrupted.
"If it's a boy." Stuart finished, playing with her.
"Oh." Helen exclaimed.
"Anyway, back to the file," said Richard realising time was running out.
"Yes, the file has a final five minutes that you need to keep as proof I am telling the truth regarding the afterlife. You must not use it until 22nd January 2212 when you can listen to it for the final time."
Richard was saddened as it meant that this would be the last time he would hear his grandfather for nearly two hundred years. What was he thinking? That was incomprehensible.
"I know you are having trouble getting to grips with the thought of living that long, but trust me, it will be very easy, very good for you both and everyone who enters the programme. Life without the woes of old age, and the ill health that brings, will be wonderful. I wish I could have known it. Beyond that there is more, much more and that is not to be forgotten either. You will have a wonderful life together and it is only just beginning. You have much to achieve but it will be worthwhile, you will see. Now I must sign off, good luck to you both, not that you will need it as you already have it. Goodbye Helen, until another time my Grandson, goodbye."
Helen switched the system to standby. Richard did not want to believe that he had gone; but the faint hum of

the system told him he had. The file had somehow stopped with exactly 5 minutes of playtime left on the countdown to the end of the file. He walked across to the system, was tempted to press play again but resisted. He knew that for the next two hundred years at least, he was in charge.

The following day, they were again waiting for a phone call from Michael. The Lords were debating the Bill. They did not have to wait too long as shortly after lunchtime the phone rang. Richard answered it immediately. Michael told him the Lords had agreed the Bill too with little debate apart from one exception. Lord Delahough had felt the need to speak. It was rather funny really. Michael said he had just sent an email through to Richard so he could see the Lords' reaction. Richard thanked Michael for all his help, and suggested that they should meet in the near future so he and Helen could buy him and his wife dinner to show their appreciation. He put the phone down and turned to Helen who had been trying to listen in. Richard filled in the gaps and they moved to the computer to read the email.

Dear Richard,

The following is an excerpt of the debate in the House of Lords. I don't think you will have many rebels here, this man is mad.

'My Lords, this proposal is monstrous; it flies in the face of morality and will bring nothing but ruin and damnation.

As in the Peasants' Revolt of 1381 in the reign of King Richard II, we will have a revolution, but this time, if this Bill is to be believed, they will do so with intelligence. Never before has an uprising by the peasants been untamed, but never before have the peasants been intelligent, that is why the Lords have always maintained their supremacy.'

At this point, a young Lord stood up to quell this nonsense, he said,

'My Lord Delahough, so you believe the peasants are revolting. Didn't someone say that in a film, ah yes, it comes to me now, Mel Brooks.

There was uproarious laughter at this point and the young Lord continued,

'My Lords, it is my view that we should go with this proposal as to do otherwise would be folly because if we do not accept it, it will happen in any event.

I put it to the House that this motion be carried.'

And, Richard, it was carried almost unanimously. Not exactly agreed, but accepted as a fait accompli.

Best Regards, Michael.

This was fantastic news to them both, not exactly unexpected, but nevertheless they now had all the approvals that they needed. Without hesitation and after only a few congratulatory kisses between them,

Helen telephoned Hans to let him know. Richard already had the first SHINE Centre at the National Hospital for Neurology and Neurosurgery and indeed all the negotiations had been complete for a while for a research centre there masquerading under a pseudonym. However, now that they had Government approval there was no further need to disguise the real proposals. In fact disguise was probably no longer possible as the press had gone into orbit with this story since the Government's approval. There were cries of everything from 'Man Plays God' to 'who will empty the dustbins now?' A large contingent of paparazzi had gathered outside the hospital gates waiting for Richard, Helen or Hans whose names had been leaked by someone at Parliament just as the recess commenced. Convenient, thought Richard, whoever it was can now keep his or her head low for three months whilst the dust settles. They could not hide forever and needed to go about their business setting up further SHINE centres countrywide, so they decided to prepare a further press release. Richard also required space to participate in the intensive training for the next week or so until his race in the Olympics. They decided to give the public, who after all would be affected by this if they chose to be, sufficient and honest information. This would allow them to start debating it amongst themselves in preparation for the questionnaire that was planned for August to see who wanted to be included in the base alteration programme. They needed to explain that unlike a computer memory upgrade, that if necessary was reversible, this was not. There was no going back. By the same token they needed to assure the public that there was no danger from this. They also had to explain in very honest terms that not everyone could benefit from it. This, they realised, would be the hardest part to accept for some and of course not everyone would know if they could be hypnotised as they might never have had the opportunity in the past. Initially the decision would not be related to extended life. That would become 'on offer' later; but it was enough at present to decide if you would want to increase your brain capacity many fold, if your partner for life or child could not. On reflection they decided not to release a press statement on its own. They also produced a guide booklet of only eight pages and a website that could be referred to for further information. This was issued contemporaneously with a press release of as few words as possible so the press could not twist it. Within the booklet, as well as a written application form, there was a reference to a web page for application to join the programme, but there was a precursor to that which was a trial hypnosis to see if a person was receptive. The booklet also advertised for hypnotherapists. There would be a need for teams up and down the country to undertake this massive programme and each of them would need to be accredited as suitable to practice.

This done, Richard had to get away. He had been so wrapped up in all of this for the past few months he felt he had neglected his training, although in reality he had actually trained well but mainly on his own. The Rowing Club chaps were also quick to point this out. However, he was lucky that he was very fit and with the type of physique that almost maintained itself providing he didn't overdo it on the food or drink front.

Nonetheless, it was now time to concentrate on the training, serious training. Hans would organise the hypnotherapist vetting and Helen the return of applications. Both would need staff and offices. One last job for Richard before he left was to set up the funding. He left the hospital to return to his flat to review the file his grandfather had given him relating to the investments he should make. He had been investing for a while now and was building funds nicely, but he needed to step it up a gear; all of this was costing tremendous amounts of money and the promised Government funding would take some time to filter through. Richard took himself away from the mêlée of the business battle and turned himself into a virtual recluse training almost constantly, fine-tuning his performance, until the day of his scull race.

The day of the race finally arrived. Everyone who was anyone was in attendance in the visitors' box on the water's edge at the finishing line. Helen, who was beginning to feel neglected, although understanding how important this was for Richard, had seen him fleetingly earlier and had kissed him for luck. Richard had already won all his heats and was now in the final. He was ready, as ready as he had ever been to take part in such a race. He was as focused as a viper about to snare its prey. His goal was clear and he wanted it desperately. Over the course speaker system he could hear that his teammate had just won the women's single scull. That made him more determined than ever; a British double was what was required. He lined up and surveyed the course, then his competitor for one last time. Suddenly, to the crack of the starter's pistol, they were off. There were large screens up everywhere for the spectators to see the two-kilometre race. His opponent edged slightly forwards of him in the first few strokes of the race, but Richard knew that this was not a problem; there was a long way to go. Six minutes of pumping his biceps and triceps and every other muscle that his body had, they were ready, there was time; he knew it. The crowd were raucous but Richard was oblivious to them. He had that finishing line in his sights and he meant to get there first. Suddenly, Helen flashed into his mind. Yes, he thought, I have to do it for her, my future wife. At that thought, his strokes increased in power and length. He started to pull level with the other scull. For about the first seventeen hundred metres they were neck and neck. Richard didn't take his thoughts off the finishing line. He knew he should not, but he looked over his shoulder. He spotted Helen in the crowd dressed in the red he had seen her in earlier. This momentary lapse cost him a few metres. Then, regaining his focus, realising there was only about two hundred metres to go, he stepped up the power. For Helen, he thought to himself, "For Helen," he cried forgetting himself. He edged back to within a few centimetres of the other scull. But his adversary must have had his own 'Helen' for he edged back again away from Richard's craft. There were only fifty metres left to go. Richard, with all of his energy concentrated on pulling his oars. Slowly he edged ahead of the other scull. He was on the brink of greatness with only ten metres to go. Could he hold on, could he keep his lead? Yes, he made it. He was first, only one can win and today it was him, the victor, by less than half a metre but so what? He had won gold. A British double in the single sculls. His American opponent was devastated, and, as usual, no one wants to know who came second; all the praise was for Richard, his moment, and his time. As he pulled up at the jetty exhausted, his teammates lifted him out of the water, boat and all. He raised himself out of the craft as well as his shattered muscles would permit, to see Helen standing next to him with her arms out.

"Richard Harper, I am so proud of you," she said. "Gold Medal man, let him through, make way," she continued helping him through to the podium to collect his medal, but not before he shook hands with his opponent, who also looked utterly exhausted.

"Well done buddy, you beat me fair and square."

Richard thanked him and moved on to where his parents were sitting. They were all over him, mother fussing and father pretending to get out the cigars, but not really, as he didn't smoke any more. It was however decidedly a cigar moment, so he liked to pretend. It took him back to his cigar smoking days that were now well and truly over, on his wife's orders. His father said, "Well done son, great fight back, but I wish your grandfather could have been here to see this."

Richard smiled knowingly and looked up, "He is Dad," he said, "he's here." His father of course didn't take this literally as he didn't yet know of the afterlife.

After the ensuing party and festivities were all over, back on planet reality, Richard settled down to business. Helen and Hans had been extremely busy whilst he was off 'enjoying himself' as they put it. The work was progressing; some hypnotherapists had been vetted and now had accreditation. Many people had expressed an interest in the programme; others had registered and a database was being populated; one that the government would not get their hands on so they could lose it thought Richard. They had even identified possible locations for further SHINE centres around the country and Hans, unsurprisingly, had explored the possibility of expansion to Germany. In fact other governments throughout the world, anxious that they should not be left behind in the 'Brain Gain' as it was now being called, were approaching them to offer buildings for SHINE centres so they too could be included sooner rather than later. Inevitably, the third world countries took little interest; they would prove to be a harder nut to crack. Nevertheless, things had indeed moved on, he thought, that was very good news. He was pleased with the progress and soon the process of Brain Gain could begin. He decided he liked that term; the opposite of what happened in Britain in the 1970's the Brain Drain, when top echelons left British shores in droves. Actually that sparked a thought, there needed to be a clause in the disclaimer they would ask people to sign, that early participants in the programme would not defect to poorer nations to make their fortune with their new found intelligence. He would add this to the paperwork.

18

Richard was sitting at home, a house he and Helen had bought just before they married in 2014. It was a sprawling early Victorian mansion with about forty rooms, a long tree-lined driveway and a gated entrance with a small gatekeeper's cottage adjacent the gate. The garden comprised about thirty acres and had been designed by Capability Brown. Robert Adam had designed the house, but it had been in a very sorry state when they had bought it. It, or rather its previous owners, had been a casualty of the 2008-11 recession and had let the place run to wrack and ruin. They had owned a string of retail outlets selling luxury goods and their business died, almost overnight, as people stopped buying their wares. Helen and Richard had picked the house up from the Official Receiver appointed to deal with the family's bankruptcy and, over a ten year period, had lovingly restored the property and its gardens to it's original splendour. For their wedding reception however, as the house had still been a wreck, they had a small area of garden restored and one room, the ballroom, a large double height space with gilt work to the cornice, oak panelling and an oak dance floor. Beforehand they had had a simple marriage service at the local village church. Then it was a short hop to the reception at their house where there were servants waiting on the guests.

Richard looked around the morning room. It faced east and the sun was streaming through the bay doors that looked out onto the rose garden. This was his favourite room of the entire house. What a splendid room, he thought to himself as he smiled and sighed with pleasure looking at the birthday cards that were scattered around the various surfaces. After a few moments, he returned to his tablet. He was reading the Sunday Times. In it was an article that he had written chronicling the Brain Gain. That name had stuck and was now to base alteration as Hoover had been to vacuum cleaner. He had been asked to do this for the younger readers, those who twenty years ago were really too young to have known what happened to them when they were base altered; their parents giving consent at the time. Richard, ever mistrustful of newspapers, decided to read the text carefully to see whether they had altered his wording.

With three hundred SHINE centres in the UK, each of which had between four and twenty hypnotherapists, it took a little over four years to complete the base alteration process for the whole country.

There were of course some that could not take part, approximately 10% of the population of the world. There were others, mostly the elderly or infirm, who chose not to take part that comprised another 5%. Thus about 85% of all humanity underwent the hypnotherapy procedure to increase their brainpower by up to nine fold. Most of those who refused the early therapy have since died leaving about 90% converted.

Following on from that, in 2017, SHINE announced the second major advance, that of increased life span whereby a second base alteration gave people the ability to live for much longer, up to a thousand years. This was of course greatly welcomed by those who had already gone through the initial programme. It gave them time to use their new brainpower and to continue learning. However, this was not so for the ones who had not been able to be base altered due to their inability to be hypnotised. Indeed, it caused more of a commotion than the original Brain Gain despite the fewer numbers that were affected. It is one thing being of a lesser intelligence level, quite another, most thought, to be denied the greatest gift of a longer life.

It was therefore an extraordinary breakthrough in 2018 when SHINE discovered the gene group that was responsible for blocking hypnotherapy on the people, who until that point in time could not be base altered. By redesigning the procedure we were then able to encompass them too, dealing with both Brain Gain and extended lifespan under the same procedure. So by then, throughout the world, almost 100% of people, who wanted to be, were converted.

The SHINE foundation continues its good work and still operates, but now on a much smaller scale in the treatment of mental illnesses and disorders that can be changed by the double hypnosis procedure and of course to base alter new life. It's now a routine matter for foetuses to be given the therapy through their pregnant mothers with an amazing success rate despite the rogue gene group that is overridden when the foetus is accessed through the mother.

Future developments are...'

Suddenly and violently interrupting the peace, the morning room door flew open with a crash like a crack of thunder as it struck the adjacent dresser. Richard looked up startled, his concentration well and truly interrupted.
"Daddy, daddy, daddy," shouted the little boy as he ran towards Richard.
"Take it easy lad, you'll knock the house down," he said trying not to laugh. "What's up Stuart, what's so important?"
Suddenly distracted, the little boy spotted a birthday card next to his father. Stuart picked it up.
"Oh, I've not seen this one before, it's from Hans."
"Oh yes, what does it say?" enquired Richard.
"It says, Daddy, 'Happy Birthday Stuart, how does it feel to be three years old?'"
"Well, how does it feel?" asked his dad.
"Oh, you know, it's just great Daddy, but I wish I was older, you can do really fun things when you're older you know."
Richard laughed heartily; his son always made him laugh.
"Anyway, Stuart, what can I do for you? What was so urgent a few moments ago, eh?"

"Oh, yes," Stuart said, remembering why he had come in, following the distraction of the card.
"I have a project to prepare for school and I need your help please, Daddy."
"Certainly, what is it?" Richard enquired.
"You remember last week we had to research digital UHD cameras," said the young lad.
"Yes, Ultra High Definition cameras, I remember."
"Well, now they want us to show how these are used in hologramavision!" exclaimed the boy, obviously fazed by this new work. Richard laughed again.
"Don't worry son, I'll explain it to you."
Just then, Helen walked into the room looking very perplexed and slightly exhausted carrying a six- month-old in her arms.
"Ah, there you are, you two; we've been looking for you, haven't we Lauren?" she said as she looked towards the baby. "This house is so big it's taken me ten minutes to find you. I'll be glad when this one can walk."
The baby looked up at her mum, "I'll be glad when this one can walk too mummy," she said.
"Okay," said Richard to Stuart as he rose to kiss his wife, "I'll help you with your project on hologramavision or HMV, if you teach Mummy how to use her Applecom properly. I know she's not that interested in technology, never has been, but the Dropdrone would be perfect for her."
Turning to his wife he continued, "It will take you back to the days of physical messages. Notes that can be personalised or even gifts can be sent by the miniature bird drones."

"Yes, Mummy it's a great application." Stuart said, reinforcing Richard's passion for this gadget.
"If you both say so," Helen sighed, feeling a little brow beaten but agreeing, as she did not want to dent Stuart's enthusiasm. Now looking at Stuart and kneeling down beside him, Richard said, "So, do we have a deal little man?" He held up his hand a little for a high-five.
"Deal!" exclaimed Stuart, slapping his little hand onto his father's.
"Okay," said Helen, trying to sound resolute but then adding, "but you know what I'm like with technology."
They all laughed at Helen's expense as Richard said, "You'll be fine, and Stuart will be a good teacher."
"Okay", she replied reluctantly. "Anyway, what I wanted you both for is lunch. It's ready. Fortunately it's a salad or it would have been ruined."
They all trouped out to the dining room where the table was set ready for them.

After lunch, Richard sat in his study with Stuart and started to explain the workings of HMV.
"Okay, son, you know how a camera works."
"Yep," said Stuart eagerly.
"It's yes you are looking for, not yep."
"Sorry Daddy, I meant yes."
"Right, holograms. They have moved on massively in the past 20 years and before that I remember when I was young, maybe 14 years old or so, going to the Science Museum and seeing an early one, in fact it was an illusion of a hologram because it was a dummy shaped like a head and clad in muslin."
"What's muslin Daddy?"

"A white cloth, like a sheet," Richard continued. "Onto that four cameras were trained with a focal point approximately equal to the distance from them to the model. The result was what looked like a head no-matter where you viewed it but it was very crude and not well focused, and very primitive, but I suppose it was the best of its time and it showed the faults we needed to address to improve upon it."
"What was that Daddy?" Stuart asked eagerly.
Richard could see that Stuart was captivated with interest. How amazing, he thought. In the future, people who did not know how children developed before the Brain Gain would take all of this for granted, but to Richard it was extremely special, that his little lad had this much ability at only three. His IQ had been tested and at 298 it was even higher than his father's.

Richard, thrilled to be having this contact with his son went on, quite lachrymose at the thought; "For Holograms to work you need projectors with variable focal points and something for them to focus onto, a moving target. The first is easy; all that was needed was a marriage between a laser and a projecting camera. The laser is so fast that it can offer all focal points over a range so that when the projection hits the target it's in focus, even when the target is not flat."
"I see," said Stuart taking it all in and looking very serious. "But how did they achieve a moving target?"
"Pressure waves, son," said Richard. "Pressure waves are sent from a flat square secretor on the floor to a mirror image receiver on the ceiling. The atmosphere at the four sides of the secretor forms a box that retains the atmosphere within it."

Realising this was complex; he started drawing a sketch to assist his son to understand the technology. What he drew was a cube. Each edge was the same as the height from the floor to the ceiling.

"You see," Richard said, hoping Stuart did, "within the cube the atmospheric pressure is manipulated to create an invisible 3-d image that you can then project onto. It's only pressurised air that forms the target or 3-d screen."

"I think I get it Daddy"

"Come with me," his father said and they walked through to the media room.

There, Richard commanded the system on and to go to their HMV. Instantly, a hologram of the news appeared at the end of the room. It was as though the newsreader and her desk were in the room.

"Never do this without eye protection," Richard said to Stuart handing him a pair of anti-laser glasses. "Okay, Daddy," he replied, donning the glasses. Richard took Stuart's hand and led him into the Hologram. Stuart flinched as he walked in but nothing happened except for a bit of tingling which was the altering pressure-waves playing on his skin.

"It tickles." he said laughing, running out of hologram.

"That's the pressurised atmosphere moving, it's harmless, but remember the laser effect is not."

At that moment, Helen came into the room with Lauren on her hip, just in time to see Richard follow Stuart out of the Hologram.

"I see you've introduced Stuart to the HMV then," she said smiling, thinking of all the fun he would have playing interactive games from inside the Hologram. "I don't understand it, but it is fun." she said.

"Yes it is; can I have another go Mum, please."
"Yes, go on then, but then you must write up your project," she replied, "and never forget your glasses. If you do, close your eyes and walk out."
"Okay, thanks Mum," he said jumping back into the invisible frame.
"And don't forget you have to teach your Mum about Dropdrone," added Richard, but Stuart was having far too much fun now to take any notice.

Later, it was Helen's turn to learn something. Stuart ran into the Kitchen where his mother had just finished feeding Lauren. He told her to get out her Applecom which, after some searching, she fished out of her handbag. He took it from her and quickly added the Dropdrone icon to the screen and said, "Dropdrone." The programme loaded up instantly. He then linked the application to her Twitter contacts, a programme that after twenty-five years, she had managed to master.
She looked on perplexed. "It's okay, Mum, you don't need to do what I just did, I've set it up for you, all you need to do now is say 'Dropdrone' to load the programme, just like I did. Now when you want to find someone just call out his or her name."
Stuart spoke and said, "Richard Harper," and immediately the screen zoomed into a location near their house and then zoomed in again to their house showing someone moving about just outside with the nametag 'Richard Harper' next to him.
"There you are, he's in the garden to the north of the house," Stuart said. "Now if you want to send him a personal note or a small gift, call up a drone."
"What do you mean, call up a drone? Helen asked.

"Look." Stuart pointed to the Applecom screen showing his mother an icon that was labelled 'Dronecall'. "You can touch this icon or say the word; it's up to you Mum."

He continued with his lesson feeling very proud of himself as he called out, "Dronecall."

"Now what?" asked Helen; who was not known for her patience.

"Here it comes."

Stuart pointed out through the open doors to a little black dot in the sky. His mother was just about to say, 'Here what comes?' as a tiny bird like object stopped about arms length from Helen at shoulder height. Helen flinched as it stopped and Stuart laughed at that.

"Land," Stuart said and the little drone spun a complete circle and moved to a chair back where it perched and said "Drone 200455, ready to accept your delivery to Richard Harper." As it said this, a small flap in its stomach opened revealing a cavity. Helen was both amazed and amused.

"Okay Mum, write a note for Daddy." Helen picked up a pen, found a scrap of paper and wrote, 'My first Twitter message delivered by Drop drone'. Stuart took it, folded it small, and inserted it into the drone.

"Wait a minute." Helen said, reaching for a mint imperial, Richard's favourites, and inserting that too into the mini cargo bay.

"Go and deliver drone 200455."

The tiny craft lifted, turned about and sped off into the distance through the open doors to the garden.

"There you are Mum, done." Stuart said grinning from ear to ear, obviously pleased with his tutorial.

Helen, impressed, said, "As easy as that, eh?" Knowing it wouldn't be for her. She bent down and warmly kissed the little lad on the forehead, "Thank you Stuart." He skipped off, still all smiles, saying, "That's okay Mum, see you later, I'm off to find Daddy," leaving his mum and Lauren in the kitchen, Helen pushing the touch screen on her Applecom and talking to it.

Stuart found his father in the garden, not far from where the Applecom told him he was located.
"Hi Daddy, how's the sweet?"
"Lovely thank-you, was that your idea?"
"No, Mummy's actually; what are you doing?"
"Oh, I'm just watching over the new Heli-trimmer. Look it's cutting the hedges without anyone controlling it."
"It looks like my helicopter, but I need to control that with a remote, how does it work?" the lad enquired.
"Well it's preloaded with a GPS fixed topographical map for our gardens, then, I set it up by adding the height and girth that I want the hedges to be and the frequency of cut and away it goes. Brilliant isn't it?" enthused Richard, as his son had about HMV.
"Well nearly, but I like to control my helicopter. It's fun making it do what I want it to do," the little lad replied, looking slightly underwhelmed.
"I'm going back in now, got to finish my project. See you later, Daddy."
"Bye, Stuart," Richard replied, watching the apple of his eye disappear into the house. He's a fine lad, he thought, and one day I'm sure he will be famous, just like his namesake.

Richard sat down on his favourite garden bench, outside his favourite room and he continued to watch his new favourite mantoy, the Heli-trimmer hovering like a large industrious humming bird, going about its business, cutting hedges. As he sat there daydreaming, he thought how lucky he was to have such a wonderful family, life was just fantastic, everything had worked out exactly as his grandfather had said it would and a slight tear came to Richard's eyes as he thought about his grandfather. Richard pondered on this for a while. He suddenly started to worry. Everything he had tried to achieve had come about. Granted, his grandfather had died but that could not be changed at the time and in fact lead to all the changes. His uncle had died too but that was as a result of an accident, something that could still not be prevented. But everything else he had attempted had come off. He was beginning to doubt this state of perfection and whether it could continue. Normally he was very upbeat, his personal motto being 'A problem is not a problem until it is here'. However, he was now wracked with worry and he felt a dark cloud had formed over him.

19

Richard and Helen's life was good, they had been together for over 100 years yet they still were deeply in love with each other and they now had quite an extended family. They were contented despite being told by Stuart that fate was predetermined. They were fortunate in that they did not need to work and their time was taken up with many good causes where they donated their time for nothing. Helen in particular was vociferous in her charity work. Richard however, had many hobbies and one of these was his cars. He still had his 1999 Aston Martin DB7 Vantage Volante in British Racing Green. It was in pristine condition and despite its years still looked new. He continued to use it even after the introduction of more modern means of transportation. Nuclear fusion had transformed the fuel industry and had assisted in protecting the planet. However anyone who was anyone had a petrol driven motor, they were all the rage, and not cheap. New cars were all run on NF but he still loved his Aston. When the last of the world's oil was used up in 2052 Richard was undeterred. He and his father simply worked out a chemical formula for petrol and created a non-polluting substitute, Harpetrol, the source of his family's income after he gave up playing the investment markets. His company, Harper Petroleum, was one of the top companies on the stock exchange and they had bought out EP at their demise. EP and other fuel companies had for many years held back development of alternative fuels to replace fossil fuel, intending to implement them before oil actually ran out but they got the timing wrong and as patents expired, the companies fell by the wayside when it did run out, leaving them vulnerable. Richard had simply stepped in, keeping all the staff and started production of his own new fuel. The demise of fossil fuels was a blessing as it turned the fortunes of the planet, which previously had been on a collision course with disaster as surely as an apple falling from a tree in autumn. Richard had not known how serious the situation was when he embarked on the SHINE programme, and his grandfather had assured him everything would work out so he trusted that. Nonetheless the pressures of population expansion were now beginning to tell on the planet and SHINE needed to reconsider their programme for land and sea expansion. Richard decided he should go back to work at the SHINE facility to lead the review of how they could accommodate all the new additions born since 2012, and how they would cope with the many more that were to come. He started making notes to remind himself of the issues he felt he would need to cover when he met his colleagues at the SHINE facility.

1 Colossal steps forward in science and the resulting innovative farming techniques that would have been impossible before the Brain Gain. The deployment of slightly convex Satellite mirrors and vast sunshades situated 22,600 km into space and circumnavigating the Earth either directing or shading the sun to previously dark or sunburnt areas assisting in ensuring famine is a thing of the past. Mini climates created by man where and when needed, 24-hours-a-day sunshine, increasing plant and food growth.

2 Religious differences are now accepted as a result of people's vastly improved understanding of one another and acceptance of differences rather than seeing them as a threat means, there is no longer any war.

3 Serious terminal disease is also relatively under control by DNA manipulation under double hypnosis.

As a result of those three issues alone, natural population control no longer happens. Whilst that is of course a good thing, it further increases the pressure on the Earth's space and natural resources.

There are of course tragic natural accidents still, after all, man cannot control nature, well, not fully, but the losses from those occurrences are negligible and make little impact upon reducing the population. It will be several hundred years before the population will stabilise as people reach their terminable age and die off naturally.

In the meantime, there are those who were already quite old, as old used to be, when the base-alteration increased their lifespan and they will die when their originally remaining years, multiplied by about ten, expire. Some who were very old when the base alteration programme took place have already died. But that number is also quite negligible and will be on a reducing basis until the last of those altered after birth has gone, leaving only those born after the life enhancing base-alteration programme with about 800 years or so ahead of them.

No, he deliberated as he sat back in his chair; he needed to return to deal with this issue before overcrowding became a problem. He continued making his notes.

The revival of space exploration in 2050 has helped. Fusion has transformed space travel so it is now viable to journey the huge distances to other planets in a fraction of the time it took in the late 20th century. There is now a vast colony on Mars that has assisted in relieving potential overcrowding on Earth. However, not everyone is comfortable leaving Earth for a manufactured existence.

The more he wrote, the more he felt it his duty to return to work to explore the alternatives. After all, he had created this brave new world, it was up to him to make sure it worked. In fact, he was looking forward to the challenge; it had been a while since he had put his still superior intellect to work. Also, he had never really thrown off his concern that everything in the world was so perfect. He had never discussed this with anyone, not even Helen, but his personal little cloud remained with him coming to the surface on occasion. The recent increase in the level of suicides did nothing to assist this. Worryingly, his grandfather had mentioned that only in passing.

No one required much sleep now, but their brains still needed time to slot away the thoughts of the day, particularly as they now had so much more power. Unusually, Richard was having a bad night. As he lay there in uneasy rest, he was beginning to wonder if his grandfather was correct and that everything would indeed be all right. He was tempted, not for the first time in the last 100 years, to hear his grandfather's voice again, but this time it was to have his grandfather's guidance and approval of what he proposed and to discuss the suicide issue. However, remembering there were only five minutes left on the recording and that his grandfather had said, "You must not use it until 22nd January 2212 when you can listen to it for the final time," he resolved not to listen to the last of the file. He determined that his best course was to re-listen to the previously played part of the file to see if it gave him any pointers as to how he should plan for the future growth of humanity and to see if he had missed anything. Leaving Helen asleep, he crept downstairs, passing the bedrooms of his great-grandchildren, Madeleine and Robert, for whom they were babysitting that night. In the kitchen he made himself some tea and moved quietly into his study where he settled into his deeply buttoned, red leather wing chair. Once comfortable he set the file to play via the remote in the arm of the chair.

"Richard .... yes it is me and I am fine. Very dead in your understanding of the word but fine none the less, please don't upset yourself, don't worry about me. You

see I am in the next stage of being, beyond life as we knew it, it does exist, the after life."
Richard drew breath sharply, it had been a long time since he had heard his grandfather's voice, but it was no less comforting than before and made, him feel surprisingly secure. He continued to listen, to the old man's voice, suddenly realising that it was now he who was the 'old man' at about 50 years older than his grandfather had been when he died. As Richard reviewed the file, he realised that everything his grandfather had said would come to be, had come to be and everything he said would be okay was okay, so he had no reason to doubt it now, did he? He carried on listening but nothing that was said really gave him any ideas about how to deal with overpopulation, or suicide. He switched the file off as it reached the previous stopping point, leaving the final five minutes to be played in 2212 when his grandfather said he should, and sat back in the chair reflecting on how they had got to this point.

"Oh, there you are Richard," said Helen walking into the study, making him jump. "Couldn't sleep?"
"No, my mind was working twenty to the dozen; it's this population issue that's bothering me, and the increasing suicide rate."
"I thought it might be," she replied, "you've been preoccupied for some time."
"Have I? Sorry," Richard offered, "any ideas?"
"Actually," Helen said, "I've been thinking about it too and I can't help remembering the lucidity you had when you told me how overcrowding might be avoided. It was before you were base-altered so perhaps it may

need modification now with further and better thought."
She sat down next to him on the arm of his chair. "When you first told me about base alteration and double hypnosis you also had ideas about how to overcome overcrowding." "Go on," Richard said.
"You told me that the planet was not overused. It was only our, then current, technology and farming methods that let us down and that we only used very little of the space available. That's now been corrected and the earth supports about three times as many souls as it did in 2012."
"Yes but it will not be long before we are at saturation point again, there is no more land and we still need more support from that land," replied Richard.

Helen went on, excited that she could remember something he could not, "Your vision was that the seas could be built upon with massive structures similar to oil rig platforms supporting new lands above the water line. You said that if you were to take a globe of the earth and trace the outline of the main continents, cut those shapes out and invert them so North is South, they would all fit into the existing sea areas and still leave one third of the globe as sea, thus doubling the land mass of the Earth. You also thought we would discover new materials far stronger than those which existed then that would be able to span further and support more load with column shapes that would not affect the underwater currents or the environment, perhaps even mesh with nature. You must remember that conversation Richard, don't you?"

"That was a hundred years ago!" Richard exclaimed, annoyed that he had not remembered it until Helen had reminded him.
"I remember it as though it were yesterday," she replied teasing him slightly, but aware of the gravity of the subject.
"Yes, I do remember now," Richard said, "What would I do without you? You're brilliant."

And she was. That entire issue was solved in one conversation with his wife. For once, he was very pleased that she had a memory like an elephant. He hugged and kissed her as they sat on his chair, grateful for her input, but also because he loved her so dearly and sometimes he forgot to show her that, but he was remembering to now. Discussing the suicides could wait for another time, he thought.

They moved from the study back to their bedroom for privacy, but Madeleine and Robert, had other ideas. They had moved, to their great-grandparents' bed where they were fast asleep. Richard and Helen had to laugh; all thoughts of passion set-aside for now, they joined the children in bed perchance to sleep for an hour or so before it was time to rise again. In the morning, Helen was up first, making tea for herself and Richard and breakfast for the children. Richard had slept and had dreamed about the plan to build a second artificial landmass equivalent to all the land on Earth, Planetwo he would call it with the original natural landmass Planetone. After breakfast he retired to his study. There was much work to be done. These would be the biggest structures man had ever contemplated.

He needed to recruit a team of experts in the fields of engineering, science, marine biology and botany. The plan needed to be completed within six hundred years, but be capable of sustaining some life within the next hundred years or so to avoid a meltdown of the human race. There were still many unanswered questions but he knew that man now had the ability to tackle such a gargantuan programme. It was, in any event, crucial that they did. The survival of the human race depended upon it.

20

Richard's plans were now well under way. There were some almost incomprehensible technical issues, particularly relating to material strength, but some of the greatest minds in the world were on Richard's team, so gradually these were being addressed. However, the bigger challenge was in dealing with environmentalist groups that were now forming on every continent. Until now, they had been ridden over roughshod by all governments, but this latest idea, to alter planet Earth, was more than many could stomach. As Richard proposed the changes, protest marches were also being planned and executed, sometimes with devastating results. Social unrest was again beginning to become an issue, something not seen for over a hundred years. Again the level of suicides jumped, reminding Richard that he never did have that conversation with Helen on the subject. Now however he needed female input, someone to assist him who had more compassion than he. As always, Helen had the answer.

Arriving home from a trip to London after a gruelling meeting with the Prime Minister, where Richard had faced more difficult questions than he cared for, he flopped into his favourite chair. Helen had heard the roof of the garage open where Richard parked his new X-Hawk, the latest six-seater personal vertical take off craft. The craft itself was silent in operation but the garage roof closing was not, allerting her to Richard's arrival. It was only late morning but Richard had poured himself a large whisky in a cut glass crystal tumbler. Knowing where to find him, Helen walked into the Morning Room to see this and immediately realised something was amiss. She sat on the arm of his chair, put her arm round his neck and said in a sincere and caring voice, "Difficult meeting, huh? Do you want to tell me about it?"

"I'll say, the Prime Minister is beside himself, he's never had to deal with anything like this, the last riots were before he was born."

"Isn't it more than that? Helen gently enquired, knowingly.

"Yes, yes it is," said Richard hesitating.

He really didn't want to have this conversation with his wife. He knew it would upset her. However, it appeared there was no choice so he continued.

"The sucide rate is now running at its highest level since the World's financial crash in the early twenty first century. I just don't understand why this is happening. Well, actually I do, but I don't know why my grandfather never mentioned the side effects of Brain Gain, he must have seen this."

Helen could palpably see his despair and she felt for him.

"Perhaps he didn't want to worry you for fear of upsetting you to the point where you decided not to champion the changes."

"No, he would have known I would go ahead; there must be more to it than that. And, what are these riots all about? I know what the issues are, but again, why did grandfather not forewarn me, us?"

Richard's, little cloud was sitting heavily on his shoulders and Helen desperately wanted to help, but she too was worried, this was not as she had foreseen it either. Richard continued, clearly thinking as he spoke, "I mean, I can see why it is happening, I just didn't expect it."

"No, neither did I," Helen replied. "But I think I can see why it's happening. It may be that people are growing into their new brains and beginning to question things more."

"No, it's not that, the troublemakers are all young, very few are older than eighty. Unlike us, they have always had brains with the higher IQ. It's as if they are the outspoken students of the late twentieth, early twenty first centuries. Tiananmen Square, the Berlin Wall and other overthrowing of dictatorships. All of these movements were perpetrated by the young, although sometimes engineered by those older and with an ulterior motive."

Helen nodded in agreement, "Yes, I see, you're right, they are growing up, the seventy, eighty year olds are the new teenagers."

She couldn't help but smile, it seemed very odd, but in the new order, Richard was correct.

Richard smiled too, realising that he had begun to have an understanding of the problem, if he had not yet

acquired the answer. "So, relatively speaking, we are dealing with either confused teenagers or militant students."
"Yes," said Helen, "but what about the instigator, do you suppose there is someone and if so who, and what can he or she possibly gain?"
"I don't know, but if that person exists, I aim to find out," said Richard, who had not touched a drop of the drink he had poured. "And, when I see, I mean speak with my grandfather again, he has some explaining to do."
He got up and hugged his wife. As always, she had helped him through his problem and with a new lease of life, he felt he could move on.

Richard moved to his study and videophoned the Prime Minister to discuss his findings. As he did so, he felt like an elder statesman mentoring a young man, similar to the way his grandfather had done for him. Just then, he realised that you cannot do it all for the young, some of it has to be from their own learning and sometimes failing; perhaps that was why his grandfather had not mentioned the riots and the suicides; or perhaps not. In any event, in the here and now it was up to Richard, the elder statesman, with a little help from his wife of course. Still, he couldn't help wondering if more difficulties were ahead that he hadn't been forewarned about.

21

Christmas 2211 had passed and the usual family gathering had taken place at Richard and Helen's country mansion. Their children travelled back to Cambridgeshire every year for the festive period to see their parents and grandparents. It was a mass exodus by some of the family from their various locations with so many family members and six generations of family, that together were over one hundred and fifty strong including friends and partners. Nonetheless, an enjoyable time and a great chance to catch up on the family's progress, new additions and of course to share new ideas. That was the best part for Richard, as he loved to hear of new exploration of space, or the depths of the seas, or new techniques for advancing human intelligence. Helen on the other hand was always so pleased to see the new additions to the family. A great time was had by all, but Richard was pleased when they had gone and he was thankful for his grandfather's foresight in suggesting a limitation on families to just two children each. 'Can you imagine', he thought, 'what it would be like if the numbers had not been limited? We would be over-run'. Indeed he was wondering what it would be like when he was seven or eight hundred years old. Even with his IQ approaching 300 he was having difficulty remembering all of their names now.

By New Year, Richard's thoughts had turned to his grandfather in the way they always did as the anniversary of his death came around. This year was however very special. In twenty-two days' time, it would be two hundred years since his grandfather had died and Richard was to be interviewed on Breakfast Hologramavision at the BBC where he would release the news about the after-life, as requested by his grandfather. Richard had prepared notes on a short tribute to his grandfather and then set about writing a speech that would inform everyone of the revelation of the after-life. His grandfather had asked Richard to wait until now before divulging the news about the after life to permit time for those who could not be part of the long life plan, and for their loved ones and relatives to have ample time to come to terms with that. He figured that two hundred years should be more than enough.

"How is it going?" asked Helen, walking into Richard's study.

"Oh, I'm nearly there," said Richard, "I'm just putting in the finishing touches. I have to say though; this is one of the hardest speeches of my life. What if they don't believe me? I have no proof."

Helen tilted her head to one side and looked at him from the top of her eye and said, "That has never been a problem for you before. You had no proof initially for me when you told me. In any case, you scientist types are always coming up with hypotheses you can't actually prove. Anyway, your grandfather thought of that as one of the reasons he wanted you to delay telling everyone about the after-life so everyone could have time to improve their IQ's and then be more open to the possibility. You also have the last five minutes of file still to play."

"That may not be enough; there are always sceptics," said Richard. "And they can cause havoc. They might think I'm a crank and that the whole thing is a trick. And all this on top of the riots; they're still going on you know."

"You," she continued, "are one of the most brilliant men in the world. They believed you when you told them about improved brain power and health through hypnosis and they will believe you now."

"Thank you darling, I can always rely upon you for support," said Richard.

"And don't you forget it," she said kissing him sweetly on the brow. "I'm off shopping now, the January sales are on, see you later."

'Some things never change' he thought, but at least now, after two hundred years he knew better than to say it to her. Richard worked on for another hour or so and then put his speech in his wallet so he knew it would be with him on the 22nd.

The next week flew by and many of his friends contacted him to wish him well. As the day approached, Richard was both excited and nervous. He decided the night before what he was going to wear, or at least he proposed some clothes to his wife and she let him decide on what he was going to wear from a reduced choice of one. Richard knew that Helen thought Richard's own choice of dress was ridiculous and that she wondered whether he would ever learn colour matching, but like him with regard to shopping, she never said anything. The dress code decided, Richard turned his attention to practical matters, how was he going to get to the studios? Helen offered to take him, but as it was a live broadcast and a breakfast show at that, he needed to be up at about 5:00 a.m. so he knew she was glad when he said "No thank-you, I think I'll stay at the London apartment. I'll drive there and I think I'll use my Aston." Richard liked this particular car because it was made when he was just 15 years old, a time when most boys are particularly impressionable regarding cars. It also reminded him of his grandfather as he had taken a great interest in the Aston despite his disability, so Richard felt it would be quite fitting to use it on the day he was to honour him. He filled the old girl up with 'Harpetrol' and sat in the driver's seat motionless for a minute or so, just taking in the ambience of the car. He thought 'what a wonderful experience' as he turned the ignition key and fired the engine with the starter button. The six litres of V12 engine roared into life. "What a sound," he said out loud forgetting he was on his own. He laughed as he thought of his wife's comment the last time he used it with her. 'What a racket, can you put the roof up?' she had said. He listened to the engine for a few minutes letting the synthetic oils warm up before switching the ignition off leaving the car conveniently positioned for his trip.

At about 6:00 p.m. Richard was ready to set off. He entered the family room where Helen was sitting and

said "Goodbye sweetheart, I'm off now, I'll see you tomorrow after my interview."
"Bye," said Helen, "and good luck. Oh, do you have your speech?"
Richard raised his finger by way of thanking her for the reminder as he took the speech out of his wallet and placed it in the top pocket of the jacket he was going to wear for the interview.
"Well done darling," he said.
They kissed and Richard left the house. He got into the Aston, smiled as it again burst into life, waved to his wife and then drove down the long driveway of their mansion to the main road. Richard reached the St. John's Wood apartment a little after eight, parked the Aston in the secure parking area under cover and walked up the stairs to his apartment. He had never given his bachelor pad up. The apartment was exactly the same as it had been when he was single and it was still in fabulous condition. It was perfectly preserved, even the multimedia system he had in his twenties still worked. He knew that for years Helen had wanted to get her hands on it to carry out a refurbishment but he wouldn't have any of it. Now the entire block was a Grade I listed building, so that idea was history anyway. No, this was his way of hanging on to reality, so much had happened over the years and this was his little retreat, his small piece of history, his grounding. After he had called home to let Helen know he had arrived safely, he fiddled around for an hour or so listening to some music and drinking tea. Then he decided enough was enough and that he should retire reasonably early, as despite the short distance to the BBC Studios in Wood Lane, he needed to be fresh. He set the radio

alarm for 4:55 a.m. and went to bed. He didn't sleep well, so he was awake before the alarm sounded. He got up at 5:15 and after the usual morning rituals and showering he dressed. Just as he was ready to go he looked at himself in the full-length mirror and thought, 'Yes, not bad for a man of two hundred and twenty-eight years'. He looked again and thought how little he had changed in the past two hundred years. Then he thought of all that had changed in that time and how lucky he was to have such a beautiful family, wealth and happiness and a wonderful wife who also had not changed much. She was still just as beautiful as she had been two hundred years ago, although she wouldn't agree. However, he was then brought back to reality as he remembered where he was going and why.

He left the apartment a little after 5:30 a.m. It was a cold winter morning, but there was no frost. It was very dark and there was no moon to assist his vision. Richard descended in the lift, opened the door to the car park and took a deep breath as he walked across to the car. The day was indeed chilly and the cold air caught his throat. He unlocked the car, opened the door and jumped in. The Aston fired up immediately, but he kept the revs down for the sake of the neighbours. He figured they probably wouldn't be as enthusiastic as he was about the sound of his engine at that hour. He set off on the few miles to the BBC Studios. The roads were virtually empty and his journey time was no more than several minutes. Nevertheless, he enjoyed the drive that passed without him even realising it, so deep was his concentration about what he was going to say at the interview. His

speech, he suddenly remembered his speech. Panicking he patted his top pocket, there was a reassuring rustle of paper and he relaxed. As he pulled up at the gates of the BBC a commissionaire opened the gate and offered to park his car for him. Just as he was about to say he would park it himself, a young girl ran to the car saying, "Are you Richard Harper? Yes you are. Thank goodness. The interviewee who was on before you has cancelled and the programme producer now wants to get you to the studio immediately."
At that Richard pocketed his key and handed the special valet key to the commissionaire and said, "Please be careful with it." The commissionaire doffed his peaked cap and said, "Yes Sir, leave it to me Sir, leave it to me. It will be ready for you when you want to travel back".

Richard followed the flustered assistant to the studio and was immediately asked to sit down on the couch in front of the cameras and lights, which he noted, were extremely bright. So bright he could not see what was going on. A make-up girl flicked round his face and then moved away. Within seconds, a young female presenter moved across the studio and sat next to him. Before he could talk the producer said, "Okay cut to Richard's interview."
The young woman said to the camera "This morning we are lucky to have Professor Richard Harper here with us on the couch. He is one of the country's leading scientists, having graduated from Oxford in 2007 and is a leading authority on theoretical physics. He is well known as assistant to Sir Stuart Harper the Cambridge Professor."

‘Presenters, they never get it right, they never do their research properly, it’s lucky they are not in science’ Richard thought. ‘I was his assistant when he was alive you dim-wit.’
She continued, “But today he is not here to talk about any of that. ‘What is she on?’ thought Richard ‘has she picked up the wrong script in the rush?’ She continued, “Well Richard, tell us how it feels to be representing your Country in the sculls race in the 2012 Olympics later this year?”
Richards’s heart started racing “What the hell….” he started to say when he noticed the daily newspaper. The date on the newspaper read 22nd January 2012. Richard was now in full panic mode. He reached into his top pocket and pulled out his speech, opened the notes and read ‘Notes for interview for Olympic entry on Breakfast TV, 22nd January.’
‘No,’ he thought, ‘how could it be?’
He pulled out his wallet and looked at a security pass for the University Campus. The expiry date was June 2012. It was then Richard realised that he was indeed there to be interviewed about his entry to the Olympics 2012, and that he must have dreamt everything about increased brainpower, longer life spans, the after-life and the death of his grandfather. He laughed to himself; his grandfather was not dead after all. It seemed so real, how could it not have happened? He looked up at the presenter who was suffering her own little panic as Richard had said nothing for several seconds and was now laughing to himself.

Suddenly and to the relief of the presenter, the programme cut to emerging headline news. *‘Terrorists have set up a booby-trapped ticket machine at the newly opened Olympic Stadium Underground Station in East London. Reports are coming in to say that the device failed to fully explode and only the incendiary device detonated.'* The report continued *'Police have told the BBC that, had the bomb been successful, the first person who used the machine after seven a.m. would have caused the bomb to explode at a time when there were likely to be many workers preparing the Stadium for the event later this year. The Station has been evacuated and closed pending further investigation.'*

Despite the news subject, Richard had managed to compose himself during this break and when the presenter looked at him and asked him if he was okay and ready to proceed he told her he was. When the camera returned to him he apologised for his confusion prior to the breaking news telling viewers that he had been getting that news before anyone else and that he was shocked. This was of course absolute rubbish but nevertheless a plausible excuse and one the presenter seemed happy to go along with. Richard continued to talk and to discuss his absolute pride in being able to represent his country in the 2012 Olympics. All previous thoughts relating to his dream were now in the back of his mind. The presenter thanked him for the interview and wished him well on behalf of the UK for his efforts later in the year. Richard left the studio at about seven-thirty and returned to his car. It was still dark when he pulled out of the BBC Studios in Wood Lane as he headed for Cambridge his mind completely full now of his dream that had seemed so real. As he reached the M11, he was still in a complete daze, remembering the files, the double hypnosis, the afterlife, the new inventions and ...... Helen. Helen he thought, my God, there is no Helen, there can't be. Suddenly, a cold chill came over him at the thought, he felt lost and hopeless.

Unthinkingly, he was speeding along at an increasingly rapid rate in a subconscious effort to get back to Cambridge to re-establish his life, when suddenly, from nowhere, a monster truck pulled out across his path. Its massive wheel caught Richard's front passenger side wing flipping the Aston into the air and causing it to fly over the central barrier into the path of oncoming traffic. Automatic roll bars instantly popped up as Richard was now upside down and looking at oncoming vehicles. Richard closed his eyes and waited, as he thought this is the end, not his grandfather's day for dying, his. As the oncoming truck hit the car, Richard winced and woke with a start to find himself in bed in his St John's Wood flat. He had awoken at the very point where he would have died. Another dream he thought, or am I dead? He was thoroughly confused. He looked at the time just as the radio alarm burst into life for 4:55 a.m. The clock must have been a little slow as the radio presenter said, *'....and we will have the Capital Radio news headlines at 5:00 a.m. in two ads time'*. Richard changed the station to Radio 4, to hear. *'This is the BBC News for the 22nd January'*.

"Yes, but which damn 22nd January?" Richard shouted at the radio.

By way of an answer, the newscaster continued, *'It is now 200 years since the death of Professor Sir Stuart*

Harper and later this morning Professor Richard Harper, his one time assistant and now renowned scientist, will be giving an interview to the BBC to celebrate his grandfather's life and to thank him for the life-changing advances he has bestowed upon us. Richard has also told us that he has something new to reveal relating to life and that he will be giving a Press Conference after the interview.' The newscaster paused and then continued with other news that Richard completely missed as he realised he was indeed in 2212 and he needed to get going if he was to make it to the BBC Studio on time. He was still rather shaken by his dream and thought about phoning Helen for reassurance but decided not to as it was so early. As he washed and dressed, Richard shouted verbal instructions to his antique multi-media system to convert the remainder of his grandfather's file to an Apple Ipod file and to send it to his Aston's hi-fi system which, also being antique, could receive such files via the old Bluetooth system.

It was still dark as he descended in the lift to the car park. As in his dream, it was a cold winter morning and there was no moon. As he reached the car park, he looked around, seeking again some sort of sign that he was living in 2212 and not 2012. Suddenly, seemingly in answer to his query, he noticed an X-Hawk lift to a hover. It was silent except for the slight whine of the rotor noise canceller. Richard watched the craft as it lifted vertically. As it reached the level of the rooftops its nose dipped and it disappeared over the roof of the flats in a northerly direction. Richard smiled as he thought to himself 'I am indeed in 2212'. He unlocked the car, opened the door and climbed in. He sat there for a second or two checking the controls, turning lights on and ensuring his file had transferred to the hi-fi system. All seemed well and as he pushed the big red start button, the Aston burst into life. He remembered his dream as he kept the revs down. This beast was no X-Hawk with its noise cancellation system. Richard pulled out of the driveway and turned towards the Studio, a journey he took slowly. On the way Richard listened to the final part of his grandfather's file. It concerned him that by using up the last of the file this might leave him without proof but then he also knew that his grandfather would know that and compensate accordingly.

"Richard", it started, "are you ready for the greatest day of your life, the day you tell everyone about the after-life?"

"Hello Grandad, I'm so happy to hear your voice again after so long. Yes, I am ready," replied Richard nervously, "but what if they don't believe me, I am now using the last of the file, where is the proof?"

"You don't really need me to prove it; most people will want to believe you particularly now that their intelligence level is so high, much higher than I could have dreamt of. After all, for centuries they have believed in the afterlife, all you are doing is telling them that it does exist. However, as proof, if you feel you need it use the way I got you to believe, tell them of a future event or better still show it to them."

"What future event, how can I show them, are you going to tell me of one?" asked Richard. "No, you are, or at least the future you is," replied his grandfather.

Richard was clearly puzzled so his grandfather continued, "whilst you are giving your press conference, an apparition of you will materialise next to you."
"What do you mean?" said Richard, now totally confused.
"Time travel, Richard, time travel. You will master it in the foreseeable future and return to today to prove that the afterlife exists."
Richard was flabbergasted; this revelation exceeded even what his advanced thought processes could manage at that moment.
"How will that prove the afterlife?" he asked. "Richard, if you tell them that you are about to materialise next to yourself and then do so you are predicting the future and that could only have come from someone who has seen it, me."
Thoroughly confused, but still rational, Richard asked his grandfather if that would not make people think that he had travelled forward in time and met his future self to tell himself he was to return to 2212 to provide evidence of the after-life?
"No," said his grandfather. "You must never interact with yourself when you travel in time as to do so would warp the space-time continuum, and you know that, or at least surmised it and it is indeed true. You can only be there and observe; you cannot affect anything, so your return can only be you returning of your own volition from the future, thus you knowing about it can only have come from someone who has told you, someone who has seen the future. Thus proof from me is not required, as your very presence from the future will validate the afterlife reality now. If you tell your audience that you will materialise, you can only know

that because I have told you that it will happen. At present you cannot know it will happen until the time when you learn time travel and can travel forward and that is still in the future for you and the rest of human kind."

Richard began to understand the concept but was now full of other questions. He thought he was going to the press conference to reveal the after-life and now he could reveal that time travel was possible to boot. He continued, "but is the world ready for this? I cannot begin to know how this works yet. For instance, if time travel exists why do we not see people who travel back? Why do we not see people from the future next to us, observing us?"
His grandfather laughed. "You want me to do your research for you, I see. Okay, think of it this way. You exist in the present time."
"Yes," said Richard knowing that he was now about to have a lecture from his mentor. His grandfather continued, "But time is ever moving forward in your world so in order to consider time travel you must stop time by considering only a point in time, a snapshot if you like. At any given point in time a person in your world is motionless, yes?"
"Yes," said Richard agreeing with this concept.
"Therefore, at that point in time they have no senses until time has passed to another future point in time where they can assess what their senses told them about what happened between the new point in time and the last point in time. This process is of course unnoticed and continuous throughout your life with millions and millions of time snapshots, which only

make sense if run together, a bit like a film with each point in time being a frame of life."

"I am with you so far," said Richard, "but what has that to do with time travel?"

"Well," his grandfather continued, "after your speech today, it was decreed by you that when time travel is learnt as a skill that it will not be done without abiding by rules of travel. The first is a rule of science and that is that interaction cannot take place, which could affect the space-time continuum. To do so could mean that you become unable to return to your own time in the future, as it may not then exist for you if you have interfered with your own history. The next rule is that time travellers must not travel back to the exact time of your present."

"I don't follow," said Richard.

"Let me explain. If you travel from the future back to your present, as you say, everyone will be able to see the time travellers. However, the people from your present time would be unable to tell if the travellers are from the present or the future. If they inadvertently interact with someone from the future it could affect the future, thus stranding the time traveller in a perpetual indeterminate state."

"So how can you time travel and not be seen?" Richard asked rather impatiently becoming aware that he was nearing his destination.

"By travelling back to a point just forward of your present time," his grandfather announced. "By travelling back to the half frame ahead in the present's future you can still see what is going on as it has just happened, but the present person's senses have not yet sensed the last frame and thus cannot see you.

Additionally, they cannot smell you, touch, taste, or hear you, as you are not there in their present time, you are in their future, but only just. You, however, can hear them as their voice sound waves take time to subside and they will still be audible."

"But what about sight, I mean the time travellers, can they see something that is in the past?" asked Richard.

"Yes." replied his grandfather slowing his speed of delivery. "There is a sense that you have not yet mastered."

Richard looked astonished at this further revelation although by now he should have expected as much.

"It is sometimes referred to as intuition, as in 'woman's intuition'. However, both men and women possess it, it's just that women are better at using it at the moment, but that will change and everyone will be able to use it in the future. Time travellers from the future are able to sense and read a person's aura, which 'lives' slightly in the future of the present, by about a frame as I have just described. Consequently, someone from the future can 'see' the aura of someone in your present and hear what they say by being a half frame ahead of their life's present time, allowing them to remain there undetected but seeing and hearing all." His grandfather continued as Richard tried to get his head around all of this.

"Richard, you will no doubt be aware of so called ghosts?"

"Yes, yes of course."

"Well they are not 'spirits' from the dead, they are simply inept time travellers who get the timing wrong and travel back to almost the same time as your present time and so can be seen by you as ethereal visions.

Sometimes they get themselves into a loop, like a bad computer programme, so they continually or perennially return to the same place giving the impression that they are haunting someone or somewhere."

Richard was silent, trying to come to terms with the latest revelations from his grandfather's file.
"Well Richard, that's about it except to say that you will materialise from the future at exactly ten a.m. two metres from the lectern and to your right. You will be in real-time so you can see yourself, don't be alarmed and whatever you do, do not interact with yourself, simply observe, comment and let your future you be proof of the information I have given you relating to the after-life, time travel and the eighth sense, the aura."
"The eighth!" Richard exclaimed, struggling to think of seven.
His grandfather laughed. "Richard, you now possess all the information I have to pass to you and it is time for me to say goodbye. Goodbye my grandson, have a good life and I will see you in your future."
"Goodbye, Grandad, goodbye."

As Richard said the words a sudden heavy feeling of emptiness and sadness came over him as he realised that he would never again be able to interact with his grandfather in this life. It was however a small comfort that in his grandfather's final words, he had told him that they would meet again. As he thought of that Richard began to wonder why he had not been able to tell people before about the afterlife as it would have made the early days of departing much easier for those who could not be hypnotised and thus could not live on.

Surely that would have lessened the hurt as family and friends passed on. Still he thought, at least they will now know so we can still ease the pain many still hold after all this time. Only now he thought I can tell them much more too and now with their vastly improved intelligence levels they will understand the reasons for delaying such news. As he turned the final corner towards the studio he realised that he had not asked his grandfather when he would discover time travel possibilities, although he figured that might be self-evident when he saw the age of his future self. At that, Richard cleared his head and started to think about what he was going to say. His prepared speech was now all but useless as not only was he about to tell the world about the after-life, he was going to divulge time travel possibilities to prove it and the existence of three more senses although one of them was still a mystery to him. In recent weeks he had considered not telling people, but he now realised after speaking with his grandfather again that the decision was not his to make. He had been entrusted to tell the world and that he must now do.

Momentarily, his mind drifted back to the riots. Neither he, nor the police, had found a perpetrator. If there was a loose cannon, he or she needed to be found and quickly. He did wonder what further response the afterlife news might spark. He was also extremely worried that all religions would need to accept that there was no religion in the afterlife. With religion being one of the biggest reasons for war over the centuries, clearly this news had the potential for further trouble. Suddenly, he became aware that he had not asked his grandfather why he had not warned him about the rioting and increase in suicide rate and he wondered what else he didn't know about that might be an issue in the future.

As he pulled up at the gates of the BBC, snapping him out of these thoughts, a commissionaire opened the gate and offered to park his car for him. Just as he was about to say he would park it himself, a young girl ran to the car saying "Are you Richard Harper? Yes you are. "Thank goodness. The interviewee who was on before you has cancelled and the programme producer now wants to get you to the studio immediately."

At that Richard pocketed his key and handed the special valet key to the commissionaire and said, "Please be careful with it."

The commissionaire doffed his peaked cap and said "Yes Sir, leave it to me Sir, leave it to me. It will be ready for you when you want to travel back".

As Richard followed the flustered assistant to the studio he looked back at the Commissionaire and smiled as he quietly said to himself, "Déjà vu."

Epilogue

22nd January 2212 - Richard reached the gates to his home which automatically detected the Aston as he approached. He travelled up the long drive, the frosted gravel crunching under the huge tyres. Swinging round the final turn of the drive he could see Helen outside the house anxiously waiting for him. He stopped the car and got out.

"You would not believe what happened when I left."

"I know, it was on the news, protesters swarmed outside the BBC while you were inside."

"I needed a police escort to get away from the car park. They had to clear a path for me, young men and women lying on the ground, it was just awful. And look at the car?" Richard pointed. "They repeatedly kicked and struck it."

"Never mind, you're okay, that's what counts, it can be fixed."

As they walked indoors Richard noticed through the media room window a still hologram of his future self on the HMV.

"It's still on the news then.' he nodded towards what he saw.

"No, I was watching it again. In fact I've walked into this projection and round the future you several times to see if you've aged. I couldn't tell, but I could see how worried you were, or the future you. Look at your expression." She pointed to the HMV as they walked closer. "I wonder what was bothering you. It looked as though you, I mean he, wanted to talk."

"Yes, I thought I looked worried. If only my grandfather was available to discuss this. If only there was more of the file."

"You don't need your grandfather's file any more young man."

Simultaneously, they spun round away from the HMV and towards the voice where Richard's future self was standing, slapping the Aston key fob into his hand. Helen drew breath sharply.

Richard held her, "I didn't know you would be back so soon, although I did expect you again, I don't know why....." He didn't finish and regaining his composure said, "So, what was it, why did you look so concerned when you materialised earlier?"

With a grim look on his face, he replied, "I need to warn you that not all is as it seems. There are some people out there trying to cause mischief for their own ends and others who feel you have cheated them of their rights."

"Who?" said Helen, finding her voice.

"I cannot tell you yet because some things that need to happen for the continuance of my dimension have not yet happened. To tell you now could jeopardise that. Suffice to say, you have much work to do to overcome various opponents to SHINE, but please believe me when I say some are prepared to kill you if they must."

"What can they possibly want?" asked Helen, her voice wavering.

"For the dangerous ones, their goal is not the continuation of mankind, their's is greed within their own lifetime. If they succeed, their control will be on a universal scale, if they fail, it will be by your efforts."

"But, have you not tampered with time, by telling us this ahead of when we should learn it?" Richard asked.

"No, this does no harm, at least not in my time, and it's imperative you are prepared. You too Helen, this is your fight too."

"What do we need to do?" asked Richard.

"All will become clear."

"Does it all work out in the end?" asked Helen.

"I can't say; too many imponderables. But if you take the wrong path, I and thus you Richard, may not exist in the future."

"When is your time, how old are you?" Richard asked, but he was leaving, shimmering to ghostly shading, then an outline and finally disappearing altogether.

Acknowledgements

Sometimes the difference between success and failure is measured only by the tiniest amount of additional effort. In this World, some people are self-driven, others need a push. In my case, on this occasion, I needed a push and it came from my wife Sheila who, when I complained of having too much to do, including having 'half a book' in my head, simply said 'so write it'. Well, as you can see, I have done just that and I'm so pleased she had faith in me. I'm not sure she knew quite what to expect though because for over five years now she has had to put up with me writing this, mostly whilst we were on holiday.

The cover design was a compilation by Sheila, who thought of the Möbius loop, and our daughter Lauren, who is the photographer/cover designer.

My editor Dan Witters has been brilliant too. Also an author, he lives in the US and is originally from New Zealand. His assistance has been fantastic including his English lessons. Also thanks to my friends, Phil Smith and Vanessa Chadwick, for the final punctuation checks.

Thank you also to Mark Pearson, for his early guidance on structuring a book and also for his kind words on the rear cover.

Why hypnosis? Well it worked for me when I used it to overcome a phobia of birds (dead or alive) and I would like to mention Phil Benjamin for allowing me to use his script as the basis of the hypnosis scenes.

I am now writing a sequel to The Greatest Gift, but don't expect an easy ride for Richard and Helen this time. As they say, when the going gets tough, the tough get going. I want the new book, 'Drifting Sands', to be out in 2013, so I guess I'll have to learn to write at times other than on holiday.

Ken Balneaves

About the author

Born in 1955 and raised in Edinburgh, Ken Balneaves attended both the primary and secondary schools of Trinity Academy. In 1971, with his father, mother and sister, he moved to Northwood in Middlesex and, save for a brief spell at Herriot Watt University, his life has been spent in that area, where he has a career in Architecture and Surveying.

Creativity is high on Ken's agenda and over the years he has designed many buildings, chiefly in the residential market, but also commercial buildings too. From a young age, as a hobby, woodwork has featured in his life, producing anything from fine furniture to general house construction.

In 2006, Ken started to learn how to fly a helicopter and believes that may be where the concept for this book stemmed, as he considered his mortality following minor incidents before and after achieving his licence.

Married to Sheila and with three grown-up children, Lauren, James and Kirk, Ken writes mainly as a hobby.